Nothing could have prepared Madi for the sight before her. As the female sea turtle began to prepare her nest, Lance whispered, "She's easily spooked at this stage so we have to be quiet."

It was touching. Inspiring. And magical. Madi swallowed past the lump in her throat. She was witnessing something that had nothing to do with being human, and everything to do with being alive.

She stepped closer to Lance and took his hand, wanting to share her wonder with him. He curled his fingers around hers and squeezed, and she knew he understood.

As they watched the turtle dig, Madi and Lance sank to the sand. "She's beautiful, isn't she?" he murmured, tenderly smoothing sand off the turtle's back. Madi watched him, her chest tight with emotion.

When the turtle was finished laying, she covered the eggs and started back to the ocean. They followed. Madi again slipped her hand into Lance's, and he twined his fingers with hers. When the waves finally swept the turtle out into the dark, endless ocean, she turned her face to Lance's, triumphant laughter spilled from her lips. Then their eyes met, and she fell silent. She brought her hands to his chest, he brought his to her hair. For a long moment they stared at each other, then Lance lowered his mouth to hers.

Madi didn't know if her heart completely stopped, or if it started for the first time. His lips were firm and strong against hers, his scent filled her head. Under his shirt his heart beat strong but not quite steadily, and she smiled, knowing he was as affected by her as she by him.

Lance couldn't get enough of her. It was as if he'd never smelled, tasted, or touched a woman before. . . .

WHAT ARE *LOVESWEPT* ROMANCES?

They are stories of true romance and touching emotion. We believe those two very important ingredients are constants in our highly sensual and very believable stories in the *LOVESWEPT* line. Our goal is to give you, the reader, stories of consistently high quality that may sometimes make you laugh, sometimes make you cry, but are always fresh and creative and contain many delightful surprises within their pages.

Most romance fans read an enormous number of books. Those they truly love, they keep. Others may be traded with friends and soon forgotten. We hope that each *LOVESWEPT* romance will be a treasure—a "keeper." We will always try to publish

LOVE STORIES YOU'LL NEVER FORGET
BY AUTHORS YOU'LL ALWAYS REMEMBER

The Editors

LOVESWEPT® · 466

Erica Spindler
Wishing Moon

BANTAM BOOKS
NEW YORK · TORONTO · LONDON · SYDNEY · AUCKLAND

WISHING MOON
A Bantam Book / April 1991

If you would be interested in receiving protective vinyl
covers for your Loveswept books, please write to this
address for information:

Loveswept
Bantam Books
P.O.Box 985
Hicksville, NY 11802

ISBN 0-553-44109-4

Published simultaneously in the United States and Canada

Bantam Books are published by Bantam Books, a
division of Bantam Doubleday Dell Publishing Group,
Inc. Its trademark, consisting of the words "Bantam
Books" and the portrayal of a rooster, is Registered in
U.S. Patent and Trademark Office and in other coun-
tries. Marca Registrada. Bantam Books, 666 Fifth Ave-
nue, New York, New York 10103.

PRINTED IN THE UNITED STATES OF AMERICA

OPM 0 9 8 7 6 5 4 3 2 1

For Stuart and Sharon Miller—
Thanks for sharing "Turtle Central" with us,
but more, thanks for being our friends.
You guys are the greatest.

And special thanks to you Sharon, for all
your help gathering information
for this book
and
for all the things we went through—
differently but the same, together
but separately.

And finally
for all the people who give their time and
energy and love to preserve these wonderful
creatures for our children
and their children.
Thanks.

Prologue

A sliver of light fell across the bed, and Lancelot Heathcliff Alexander looked hopefully toward the door. "Mommy, is that you?"

"Lancelot, honey, what are you doing still awake?"

"I was waiting for you." Lance rubbed his eyes and sat up. "How come you're so late?"

She crossed to the bed and sat down. Putting her arm around him, she kissed the top of his head. "You know Friday nights I do Dickerson Industries. It always takes longer."

"I forgot." He smiled and snuggled into her side. She always smelled so good—like soap and the lemon polish she used on the table in the living room, the one she wouldn't let him color on. "I made you something in school today."

"You did?"

Lance nodded, about to burst with pride and excitement. He loved it when she smiled at him that way, as if he were the most special boy in the world. Giggling, he reached under his pillow. The card stuck to his fingers a little, and some of the glitter flaked off when he handed it to her. He hoped she didn't notice.

"It's so pretty," she said, holding the card out in front of her. "It must have taken you a long time to make."

Lance held his breath as she opened it. Her smile disappeared and she looked funny—the way she did sometimes when she thought he couldn't see.

He blinked furiously, trying not to cry. He never should have listened to that stupid Miss Pratt! She'd told him it would be okay to make his mom a card for Father's Day and now he'd made his mommy sad!

He hung his head in disappointment. "You don't like it."

"That's not true, Lancelot," she whispered, her voice sounding rough. "I love it. Thank you."

"No, you don't, I can tell." He jutted his chin out, trying to make it stop wobbling. "You look sad."

"Oh, sweetheart." She pulled him onto her lap and hugged him so tightly, he almost couldn't breathe. He didn't tell her though, it felt good anyway. "I know this sounds silly, but sometimes grown-ups are so happy they're sad. Sometimes they even cry when they're happy."

He frowned, unconvinced. "Really?"

She rubbed her cheek against his hair. "I named you after the strongest, bravest, and most handsome knight of King Arthur's Round Table. How could you ever make me unhappy?"

Lance thought of the names that mean Rodney Willis had called him just today. The teacher had taken Rodney to the principal's office, but Lance couldn't get the words out of his head.

Illegitimate. Bastard.

Lance clenched his hands into fists and fought off tears. Rodney had said that bastards couldn't be knights of the Round Table. He'd said they didn't get to have real families either. Not ever. Lance peeked up at his mother. She would tell him it wasn't so. Then Rodney would be in even more trouble.

But what if he made her sad again? He remembered her expression of a moment ago and felt that funny, trembly sensation in his throat. He swallowed hard. Crying was for babies. Knights were big and strong and took care of their families . . . especially the girls.

Lance sat up straighter. He'd show that stinky ole Rodney the Rodent. Someday he'd show him.

"Mommy?"

"Hmm . . ." She stroked his hair.

"Tell me again 'bout the brave knight and the beautiful Gwina . . . Gwina . . ."

"Guinevere," his mother said softly.

"Yeah, and tell me 'bout the Round Table too."

His mother propped the pillows up behind them and scooted back, bringing Lance with her. Then she began, "Once upon a time . . ."

One

The breeze off the ocean contained only a hint of the heat to come. Lance Alexander—he'd long ago stopped allowing anyone to call him Lancelot—looked up from the contract on the sand in front of him and out at the solitary stretch of beach. Soon there would be surfers and swimmers and those who simply worshipped the sun, but now, in these early morning hours, the beach was almost pregnant with quiet.

He closed his eyes and breathed in, allowing himself one long moment of enjoyment. He would finish up with the contract, then have his run. After that: breakfast, the financial page, and a shower. Checking his sport-watch, he noted that he was a little ahead of schedule. This morning there would even be time for the paper's Saturday supplement.

With a pleased smile, Lance focused on the document once more, only to be distracted by a movement he caught in the corner of his eye. He turned, then arched his brows in surprise. It was too early in the day for sun-bunnies, yet here was one, striding toward him.

She wore mirrored aviator sunglasses and a string bikini. The suit's color, the vivid green of a slice of honeydew, stood out in bold contrast to the voluptuous body it did little to conceal. Her flesh was golden from the sun, smooth from pampering.

As she neared, the breeze caught her thick mane of hair. Even as he told himself to get back to the Dickerson contract, Lance wondered how those carmel-colored strands would feel twining around his fingers.

She saw that he was watching her and held up a hand in greeting. Lance silently swore and dragged his gaze back to his work.

This woman did not fit into his plans, any of them.

A moment later her shadow fell across him.

"Hi."

He looked up again. This time his gaze traveled along long, shapely legs and inch after inch of perfect female flesh until his eyes found hers, shielded behind the mirrored shades. It was disconcerting to see himself—and the contract, his portable phone, and carton of juice—reflected in her glasses. But looking away would be even more disconcerting. He knew that for a fact.

"I'm sorry," he said. "Have we met?"

"Not yet." She tilted her head coquettishly to the side, and her wild mane of hair cascaded over her shoulder.

Lance worked to keep his expression neutral.

She was trying to pick him up! It wasn't that women didn't find him attractive or come on to him, they did. But this was a sex goddess, and it was only seven-thirty in the morning.

"I saw you come down here," she continued, "and thought it would be a great opportunity to get acquainted. I believe you're my turtle connection."

She smiled at him in a provocative way, and for a moment Lance, who prided himself on his ability to think clearly in all situations, couldn't think at all.

In that moment, she sank onto the sand beside him, then held up a small white paper bag. "Breakfast," she said by way of explanation, and took from the bag a pint of pistachio fudge ice cream and a plastic spoon. "Would you like some? I have only one spoon, but I'll chance it if you will."

"No, thanks, Ms . . ."

"Muldoon," she supplied. "Madison Muldoon, your new neighbor . . . and your new fund-raiser." She stuck the spoon in the ice cream and held out her hand. "Just call me Madi."

Lance took her hand, stunned silent. This sun-bunny was the fund-raiser the Sea Turtle Society had hired? What had the board been thinking of?

He found his voice then, knowing that a second more of silence and he would look like a total idiot. He assured himself only surprise had had him tongue-tied. "Lance Alexander, the Society's director. We didn't expect you for another week."

"I know."

No explanation, nothing. Lance frowned and waited as she took several bites of ice cream. "You came highly recommended," he said at last.

"Yes, I did." She laughed. "And you came with a warning attached: skeptic at hand." She pushed at her untamed hair, laughing again. "Thanks, by the way, for making the arrangements for this condo. That's the one thing I hate about these assignments, finding a place, that is."

She talked in circles. How could a woman who did that convince businessmen to donate thousands? "I hope you like it."

"I love it." She took another bite of the ice cream, catching a drop of it with the tip of her tongue. "I expected something cold, something high-risish. This was a pleasant surprise."

"Good," Lance murmured, glancing back at the townhouse-style condominium his company had built several years before. The three tristory units faced the beach, with sliding glass doors leading out to decks on every level. He'd liked the design so well, he'd moved into one himself. The other two, including the one next to his, the one Madi Muldoon would occupy for the next year, the company had kept for clients.

She sighed and fitted the lid back on the carton of ice cream. After dropping both it and the spoon back into the bag, she stood. "The surf beckons. Join me?"

"I've got some work to do."

She slipped off her sunglasses and tossed them onto her Minnie Mouse beach towel. "I see that."

He heard amusement in her voice, amusement and something else, something that rankled. He fought the emotion off. "Perhaps we could meet later?"

"Perhaps." Without waiting for another response, she turned toward the shore, then looked back at him. "How's the water this time of year?"

"Cold."

"Too bad. I think I'll try it anyway."

Lance watched her walk away, his throat dry, his chest tight. He should get back to the Dickerson contract and his schedule. His spare minutes were slipping by, as was the morning. He couldn't drag his gaze from her, though, and he didn't really want to.

She walked slowly, lazily even, toward the ocean, pausing now and then to drag her hands through her hair or to nudge something in the sand with her toe.

When she reached the edge of the water, she stopped and lifted her face to the sun, letting it bathe her. As she did, her glorious hair cascaded down her back. Lance sucked in a sharp breath, his hands itching once again to bury themselves in the silky stuff.

She was a woman totally in tune with her own body, he thought, rolling his taut shoulders. The relaxation he'd felt a few minutes ago was gone. That ease had been replaced by arousal—gut tightening and sanity stealing.

Lance closed his eyes and took a deep, steadying breath. This was ridiculous. He was too old for a hormonal takeover. This kind of quick heat was reserved for adolescents. He was a logical, rational man who knew what he wanted.

He opened his eyes. Madison Muldoon had inched into the surf. Bending, she scooped up a handful of the water and drizzled it over her arms and chest. Lance sucked in a sharp, almost painful breath as he imagined the sting of the cold water on her heated skin—and the slick warmth of flesh against flesh.

His papers fluttered, then lifted in the breeze. He made a grab for them, catching them a moment before they would have tumbled down the beach. A picture of himself racing after them filled his head, and he shook it away. He had better get it together, and fast, or he would look like a fool as well as a voyeur.

Glancing at her again, he smiled wryly. He would like to believe Madi Muldoon was performing for him, and what man wouldn't? But as much as his ego wanted to think this woman was aware of him watching her and was pleased by his attention, he knew she had forgotten him the moment she'd walked away.

So much for being picked up.

Which was for the best, he told himself. That the Society's board of directors had chosen her fund-raiser was a problem he would have to deal with. It would be foolish to invent any other situations involving Madison Muldoon.

Madi scooped up another handful of the chilly water and let it trickle through her fingers. It felt good to be in Florida, away from the continual buzz and smog of Los Angeles. She'd chosen Melbourne Beach and its Sea Turtle Society for precisely that reason. For the first time in forever she felt like she could take a deep, calming breath. Maybe she would even start sleeping well again.

If only she could so easily escape the hollowness

that had gripped her since her younger sister Tina had announced first her marriage, then her pregnancy.

Madi closed her eyes and the smell of the hospital maternity ward—a combination of baby powder and antiseptic—filled her head. She thought of her new niece, of the way that tiny bundle of pink, cream, and gold had filled her arms, of how her arms had ached when she'd handed the baby back to her sister, and she curled her fingers into her palms.

Maybe it was her hormones. Hormones from a body that would be thirty years old in a matter of weeks.

The flutter she felt every time she thought of her thirtieth birthday settled in her stomach, and she swore softly. This had to stop. It was foolish and self-defeating. She had a great life. She was successful, beautiful, well liked. . . . She was happy, dammit, she was.

Madi frowned, then realizing what she was doing, fought off the self-doubts and regrets. She was done with them. She was done with second-guessing herself and cross-examining her feelings. Today the old Madi, the confident, resilient one she trusted and relied on, returned for good.

Breathing deeply, she tuned into her surroundings, willing the beauty of the day to work its magic on her. As the heat of the sun warmed her, she thought of the man she'd just met, the man she would be working with for the next year.

Lance Alexander—forty years old, never married, owner of Florida Coast Construction, and volunteer director of the S.T.S. for the last three years.

Before the turtles he'd donated his time to another of Florida's endangered creatures, the manatee.

A member of the board of trustees had briefed her on the people she would be working with, but a face-to-face meeting told so much more than statistics ever would. And in the couple of minutes it had taken to introduce herself, she'd sized him up, just as she sized up every man she met. Not as a possible conquest, or even a challenge. But as a potential threat.

Lance Alexander, she'd decided, would be manageable.

She almost laughed out loud. Manageable seemed, even to her, an odd adjective to pin on a man like Lance. His face was strong, his features chiseled. He held himself erectly and with confidence—the sort of confidence that came from having fought many battles and won. And despite his all-business attitude and clean-cut hair and face, she sensed a virility about him.

That was why he would be manageable. Madi tossed her head, and her hair tickled her shoulders and back. He was the type of man with whom she would never let down her guard, not even for a second.

At that moment a particularly eager wave licked at her toes. Madi squealed and jumped back. The wave followed her, and within moments her feet were swallowed. Laughing at the water's sting, she tilted her chin and changed her tactic, stepping boldly forward. This time when the wave hit, the water splashed over her knees and onto her thighs.

A fine sheen of goose bumps raced over her, and

she laughed again. She was a California girl, born and bred, and here she was in Nowhere, Florida acting as if she'd never been to the beach before. She shook her head at the irony, even as she bent low to scoop the chilly water over her arms and chest. The goose bumps spread until her nipples hardened and pressed against her bikini top.

The sensation was delicious. Feeling wicked, Madi eyed a huge wave on the horizon. Twelve hours ago she'd been racing to catch a flight out of Los Angeles International. She'd been harried, frustrated, and feeling as if life had cheated her out of something important. She tossed her head in determination. Today she would challenge the biggest wave of all and win.

She stepped farther into the water, bracing herself for the wave as it barreled onto the shore. It crashed into her, soaking her from head to foot, almost knocking her off-balance. Almost, but not quite.

Laughing at her victory, Madi pulled herself out of the water. As she did, her eyes met her neighbor's. He'd been watching her play in the surf. His expression was enigmatic, but a tingle, much like that of the cold water against her heated skin, eased up her spine. With it came awareness, aching and vibrant and debilitating.

In a split second the sensation passed. Shaken, Madi pulled herself together. She hadn't felt that way—alive and aware and totally female—in a long time. She lifted her chin a notch. She wouldn't feel that way again.

Summoning her most confident smile, she started back toward the dune. As she stopped in front of Lance Alexander, she resisted the urge to grab her towel and run for the condo. "Finished your work?"

He tipped his head back. "No, I rearranged my schedule."

She sat down next to him. "You decided you couldn't pass up this opportunity to get to know the enemy. Can't blame you"—she leaned back on her elbows and lifted her face to the sun—"although your worries are totally unfounded."

"Someone told you I voted against hiring a fund-raiser."

She didn't look at him. "Told me, in fact, that you were the only one who had and that you were adamant."

"It was nothing personal." Lance frowned out at the ocean, then turned back to her. "I have doubts that you, or any fund-raiser, could bring in the amount of revenue you promised. Not here."

She met his eyes, feeling totally in control once more. "I'm good at what I do, Mr. Alexander. And I don't promise things I can't deliver."

"That may be, but we're a small organization, Melbourne Beach is a small community. If you don't deliver, your salary will exhaust all of our available funds. You'll cripple us, Ms. Muldoon."

She tilted her face to the sun once more. "The board of trustees doesn't seem worried."

"They've never seen it happen before."

"The Manatee Organization."

"You've been briefed."

She looked at him through her sweep of honey-colored lashes. "You make it sound like I'm a spy or something."

He laughed. "Darnell Peabody, I'm guessing."

"A lovely man. I charmed him."

"I'm sure you did." Lance propped himself on an elbow. "You'll find I'm not so easily swayed."

"A tough nut to crack? That's okay." She ran her fingers through her hair; it was nearly dry. "I grew up in Hollywood. You can't intimidate me."

"I wouldn't try," he said mildly, trailing his gaze slowly, deliberately over her.

Madi smiled at his tactic. She preferred a frontal attack, herself. Standing, she held out a hand. "But you're the type of man who can't help but try. Come, let's walk and talk turtles."

Lance grasped her hand and let her help him up. She was tall, maybe five-ten, and her stride was long but somehow lazy. They walked for several minutes in silence, Lance using the opportunity to study her. Her profile was far from perfect. Her nose was too strong, her chin too sharp; her forehead was high and broad, her mouth full and pouty. They all added up to an intriguingly beautiful, if unconventional, face.

But more than physical beauty made her appealing, even charismatic. She was cocky and confident and a shameless flirt. Sensuality rolled off her; it was there in the way she moved, her voice. Sexy, seemingly without effort or artifice, she was the kind of woman who drew gazes and inspired fantasies. He would bet most men fell all over themselves around her.

He wasn't most men. Despite his earlier departure from good sense, he wouldn't allow himself to be distracted.

"So," he said finally, "how much do you know about the turtles?"

"A start." She turned toward him, holding a hand to her eyes to shield them from the sun. "I know that worldwide this is one of only a handful of nesting beaches for the giant sea turtles, and that they're endangered. The nesting season begins in May and ends in September. The purpose of the Society is to make sure the maximum number of turtles nest and as many hatchlings as possible make it to the ocean. Or, in short, you guys are around to make sure an endangered species doesn't become extinct."

She paused, and Lance shook his head, realizing he'd been listening to her as if captivated. Her voice wasn't suited to talking business. Low and easy, it brought to mind hot afternoons in cool bedrooms and chance encounters at out-of-the-way bars. It was the kind of voice that had you opening your checkbook without a second thought.

Or forgetting carefully laid plans and lifelong promises.

He frowned. This wouldn't do, not at all. They'd spent, really, only minutes together, but still he knew she wasn't what he was looking for. He dragged his thoughts back to the subject of their conversation. "We've been instrumental in getting protective ordinances passed locally and have participated in several key pieces of national legislation."

"And to your credit," she inserted, lifting her heavy hair off the back of her neck, "everything you've accomplished has been through raising community awareness and generating community involvement."

Lance followed her movement with his eyes, then silently swore and jerked his gaze away.

"I also know," she added, "that up until now, all fund-raising has been done strictly on an *ad hoc* basis, and the majority of your revenues stem from individual and business donations."

"As I said before, you've been briefed."

"No," she corrected him, meeting his gaze evenly. "I've done my homework. I'm a professional fund-raiser and am extremely successful because I'm good at what I do. I would like us to work together amicably. It will make for a much easier . . . and more productive year."

Lance inclined his head, admitting admiration. "Of course, the Society comes first. But let me warn you, Ms. Muldoon, I plan to scrutinize your every move, question your every decision. I won't make it easy for you."

"I wouldn't have it any other way." Her eyes narrowed, just a bit. "But I won't let you interfere with, or keep me from doing my job. I have the board on my side already and I won't hesitate to use that advantage."

So, she was going to play hardball. Annoyance warred with respect. "We've come to an agreement then?" he asked.

"I guess we have."

"Good."

"She started to move away from him, but he stopped her with a hand on her elbow. "One more question, Madi Muldoon. Why did you take this job?"

She looked at him, and he saw that he'd caught her off guard. He also saw that she didn't like it.

"What do you mean?" she asked.

"I've done my homework too. This is much smaller than your usual assignments and although your base salary is standard, here your ten percent on collected monies will be considerably less."

"Why did I accept this job?" she said after a moment. "What's to refuse—the beach, a beautiful condo on the water, men in bathing suits?" She pushed her hair away from her face; the breeze tossed it back. "This was too good to pass up."

He studied her, battling unreasonable frustration. She wasn't being honest with him. It shouldn't matter; he hadn't expected her to. But he also hadn't expected a glimmer of something in her eyes—something soft and the tiniest bit haunted. That glimpse of vulnerability in this otherwise impervious woman intrigued him.

He arched an eyebrow. "Really?"

"Really." Madi lifted her chin a notch, anger tinting her cheeks. "And what about you, Mr. Alexander? Why turtles? Why charities?"

"Why do you think?"

She let out a short, frustrated breath. "That's not what I asked."

"True." He shifted his gaze from hers to the ocean. "Would you believe me if I told you I love the earth with all her magic and mysteries?" He turned back to her, schooling his expression to neutrality. "That I feel not only a moral need to help preserve her, but a compelling desire to do so as well? Or even that when I look at the turtles I ache?"

Madi narrowed her eyes, studying him. "No," she said, shaking her head. "I wouldn't."

"Fair enough." He checked his watch. "Shall I accompany you back?"

"Thanks, but I think I can find my way."

"Good. I'll see you at Darnell's party Friday?"

"It's why I arrived early."

"Until Friday, then." Without another word, he turned and walked away.

Two

"Madison, darling, I'm delighted you could make it." Darnell Peabody caught her hands and brought them to his lips. "Come in, come in."

"Darnell." Madi smiled at the elegant middle-aged man and let him lead her through the doorway of his palacial beachfront home. She'd met him only twice before, but already she knew his penchant for gossip and expensive clothes, and that she liked him.

Once inside, he held her at arm's length and studied her brilliantly patterned gauze dress with the eye of a professional. Subtly sexy with its high neck and cutaway shoulders, the dress fit snugly at her waist and skimmed over her hips.

"An ingenious design, my dear," he murmured, noticing the way the ribboned full skirt exposed daring amounts of leg with each step. "You look positively delicious. If I weren't a confirmed . . ." His voice trailed off as he eyed a man wearing

Armani originals. He sighed melodramatically and turned back·to her as the man took the arm of a striking blond. "The best are always taken, don't you think?"

Madi laughed and tucked her arm through his. "Best is a relative term, Darnell."

"A cynic? My, my, I never would have guessed." He made a clucking sound as together they stepped into a Florida room the size of many one-story homes. Doors opened to the outside on three sides, leading to a multilevel terrace complete with swimming pool and hot tub. Flowers adorned every table, ledge, and corner; the air was thick with their scents. Lanterns provided festive spots of colored light, and piped-in reggae combined with the music of the ocean to complete the island mood.

"Darnell, this place is fabulous. Tell me—" She angled him a conspiratorial glance. "Just what is it that you do?"

"Not me, my dear, my grandfather." He nodded regally to a couple they passed. "He made a fortune in Florida resorts. For myself, except for my wonderful, lumbering sea creatures, I do as little as possible."

She laughed. "You're incorrigible."

"Flattery, flattery." He leaned toward her. "Have you seen one of our turtles yet?" She shook her head, and he sighed. "You are in for a treat, my dear. They are marvelous, just marvelous. Actually, I think they were a more important part of my childhood than my father, but that's another story."

Madi laughed again. Something about Darnell

reminded her of the Pekingese she'd brought home when she was ten. "You'll tell me one day, I hope?"

"Over margaritas on the beach, but for tonight . . ." He smoothed a hand over his silver hair. "I'll tell you this, there is money here tonight. Big money. The contacts could make your year."

"Or rather," she murmured, "the Society's year."

"Exactly." He looked pleased with himself. "I've been telling the board for ages that they should give parties like this and make people pay to come. They would, you know. This party *is* the event of the season."

Madi met his gaze. "I hope you won't be miffed, but I plan to outdo you."

"Not at all, my dear. I rather prefer a challenge." He grinned and looked furtively to his left, then right. "Have you met our director yet? Positively a stick in the mud."

Madi thought of Lance, of his serious, no-nonsense approach to life, and smiled in amusement. She understood why he and this gossipy board member did not always see eye-to-eye. "I have. We had a lovely chat."

Darnell snorted. "Lovely chat indeed. I have no doubt you'll bring him around, but don't be fooled, my love, the man's a shark. Now I must run. Do have some champagne."

Taking Darnell's advice, Madi helped herself to a glass of champagne as a waiter passed. She sipped, thinking of her encounter with Lance. He'd infuriated her, as much by his ability to get under her skin as by his sarcasm and skepticism.

She wasn't accustomed to being knocked off-balance and didn't like it.

She drew her eyebrows together as she took another sip of the sparkling wine. Lance's eyes, a light, clear green, had been direct and too knowing. She'd had the feeling he'd seen right through her, and that . . . there was more to him than she'd first thought.

A tremor ran through her, and she scowled. No, Lance Alexander was the shark Darnell had called him. A person didn't achieve his kind of success without a healthy dose of the killer instinct. She understood men who were driven to success at the exclusion of all else. After all, her mother married them with shocking regularity.

Madi downed the last of the champagne, then exchanged that glass for another. Tonight was for business, not for ruminating over her past, not for analyzing her colleagues. She smiled. The contacts she made here *could* go a long way toward making her year—and showing Mr. Shark Director just what she was capable of.

With that thought, Madi began to circulate, eavesdropping unabashedly.

". . . her entire trousseau done by that horrible new designer . . ."

Old money, Madi thought. And conservative. She moved on.

". . . seems to me, one can do without tuna fish if it means saving a dolphin. I for one . . ."

Liberal but without funds, she decided, eyeing the cut of the couple's clothes. Good volunteer material.

She wound her way around a group of men in a heated discussion.

". . . putting money in the market right now is suicidal. The takeover of that third world country . . ."

She lowered her gaze—one Rolex watch, one Cartier, Cole-Haan and Bally shoes. Professionals, she determined. And doing well. She smiled, made a mental note, and moved on.

". . . day-care? Of course. A woman can't be expected to subjugate herself for . . ." Career woman on the climb. Madi began to move away, then stopped as she recognized Lance's voice.

She hadn't seen him at first, as he was standing slightly behind a giant potted palm. Madi inched to her left to get a better view of him. The majority of the men had dressed casually—everything from pricey active-wear to jams. Lance was dressed as if he'd come straight from the office.

The fluttering of her pulse was a surprise, an annoyance, and Madi shook the sensation off as she studied him. For this late in the day he was amazingly unrumpled—his businessman's blue suit seemed eight A.M. fresh, his plain white shirt still crisp, the burgundy pinstrip tie impeccably knotted.

Only his thick, silvery-blond hair spoke of a dayful of meetings and petty annoyances. Slightly tousled, it tumbled across his forehead, and every so often he reached up to shove it back. Madi smiled. That tiny fault, that one uncontrollable thing in a man with so much control, was endearing. And far too appealing.

She caught her bottom lip between her teeth as

the urge to help him, to smooth back the hair with her own fingers, washed over her. And with the urge, came the oddest twinge in her chest.

She shook her head and curled her fingers into her palms. Why in the world would she want to tidy the one thing that made Lance Alexander more of a human and less of an automaton?

"But you *do* plan to have children?" he asked the woman.

Madi arched her eyebrows. Odd party conversation, she mused, especially from a man like Lance. Not at all embarrassed about listening, she took a step closer—only to be lassoed by one of the female boardmembers.

By the time she finished exchanging pleasantries with the woman, Lance was gone.

For the next couple of hours Madi worked the room, using what she'd ascertained on her first spin around to make contacts. The liberals got her open "California girl" greeting, the old money her haughty asides, and the professionals her straightforward, all-business approach.

And during that time she saw Lance with a dozen different women.

Madi drew her eyebrows together and glanced around the room, looking for him once again. Lance didn't seem the type of man who chased women, but if the number of business cards and phone numbers exchanging hands was any indication, he was going to be a very busy boy.

She released her breath in a short huff. From what she'd been able to catch, he had some of the cleverest pickup lines she'd ever heard—and she'd thought she'd heard them all. Madi shook her head. Ingenious. Who would have considered a line about the work ethic, two-car garages, or religious beliefs a prelude to romance?

"You're frowning, darling. Haven't you heard? Parties are for smiles."

Madi jumped as Darnell caught her arm. She met his eyes guiltily. "I was, wasn't I?"

"You must need more champagne."

"No." She laughed and shook her head. "No more champagne. Thank you."

"If you're sure, come, there's someone I want you to meet. Bucks," he whispered as they crossed the room. "Big, big bucks. But I must warn you, he's a tough nut to crack."

Madi thought once again of Lance. "Those types are my specialties, Darnell. Lead the way."

This had to stop. Lance sipped his mineral water and watched as Madi tipped her head back and laughed. His gaze lingered on the sensual arc of her neck, and he frowned. He had a specific goal he was working toward. It didn't include will-o'-the-wisp, sun-bunny fund-raisers.

Then why, with all the women he'd interviewed that night—interesting, beautiful women, excellent candidates all—had he kept half an eye on Madi?

Annoyed, he downed the mineral water and signaled for a waiter to bring him something stronger. Moments later he'd exchanged the water for wine and tossed back half a glass.

Madison Muldoon was dead wrong for the job.

He knew that. So obviously there was some other reason he was fascinated with her.

Not fascinated, he corrected himself quickly. Not even interested. Curious. Who wouldn't be? After all, the woman had charmed Bernard Hessman III. Lance shook his head. No one charmed Hessman, except, maybe, Hessman himself.

But Madi had the man eating out of her hand—and every other man and woman in the room. She seemed to fit in with whatever person she chose to approach. He'd seen people who hadn't cracked a smile in years laugh with gusto, people who distrusted everyone welcome her with open arms.

What was her secret?

The dress certainly didn't hurt, he thought, trailing his gaze over the peek-a-boo skirt. She moved slightly, and he glimpsed the smooth, tanned flesh of her thigh. Swallowing, he dragged his eyes back up to her face. Nor did that glorious mane of hair or her low, lazy laugh hurt—both of which she used with abandon.

Lance loosened his tie. It was more than knowing how to work a room, though, more than her gorgeous face and body that had people falling all over themselves around her. Many people had those attributes. Something made this woman special.

Assuring himself his motives were purely professional, he decided to find out what.

Lance wound his way through the crowd, catching her a moment before she stepped out onto the terrace. As she turned toward him, the scent of her perfume, at once quixotic and uncomplicated, wafted over him. He shook off its effect. "Hello, Ms. Muldoon," he murmured.

Madi's heart beat heavily. Manageable, she reminded herself, and smiled. "Good evening, Mr. Alexander."

"You seem to be doing well tonight."

"So do you."

He arched his brows. "You were going out for some air?"

"Yes."

"I'll join you."

Madi didn't balk. He hadn't asked, but then she wouldn't have refused if he had. Together they stepped out into the warm evening.

The throng of people was thickest near the house. By unspoken agreement they headed away from the building and toward the beach. They stopped on the last of the terrace's tiers before the dune.

A waiter passed. Lance helped himself to two glasses of champagne and held one out to her. As she took the glass, their fingers brushed. The accidental touch seemed oddly intimate, unreasonably disturbing, and Madi resisted the urge to snatch her hand away.

She turned toward the ocean, leaning against the stone step-wall that circled the terrace. The breeze pulled at her dress, molding it to her body. The full moon reflected cool white light off the black bowl of the ocean.

"A wishing moon," she murmured, tipping her face to its light. "My mother insisted that a wish made on a full moon would always come true."

"I've never heard that one before."

"I've no doubt she made it up. My mother has a flair for both the dramatic and for manipulating the truth. But I don't take any chances." Madi lifted her face to the moon, shut her eyes, and wished. Feeling a bit foolish at the thoughts that ran through her head, she opened her eyes and angled him the smile that had landed tougher men than he at her feet. "You really should make one."

"You're an odd woman, Madison Muldoon."

"Am I?"

"Mmm, I've been watching you tonight."

"Really?" She looked at him over the rim of her glass, amused. When had he had the time? she wondered. "I find that hard to believe."

His gaze was deadly serious. "It's true."

"And what, besides the fact that I'm odd, did you learn?"

He paused before answering. "You're not everything you seem to be. And I don't like mysteries."

"I'm not surprised." She drained her glass, then set it on the step-wall. "But I'm no mystery. Ask me anything."

He smiled. "That seems a rather poor tactic."

"You're assuming I'm either playing a game or have something to hide. I assure you, neither is the case."

"Why don't I believe you?"

She shrugged. "Not my problem." Music trickled down from the house, and she began swaying to the calypso beat. "I haven't danced all evening. Dance with me, Lance Alexander. All business will make us both very dull."

Lance hesitated, but only for a moment. Simultaneously they put their champagne glasses down on the beach. He took her in his arms and, holding her lightly but stiffly, led her to the rhythmic music.

Madi rested her forehead against his shoulder. He smelled good, straightforward, like soap and aftershave and good old-fashioned hard work. She breathed in the heady combination. Immediately feeling lightheaded, she cursed that third glass of champagne.

"You're pretty good," she murmured as he executed a tricky turn.

"Even that's an exaggeration," he said matter-of-factly. "I don't particularly care for dancing."

"Really?" She looked up at him, surprised. "What's not to like?"

He studied her for a moment before answering. "You're pushy, you know that?"

He wasn't teasing, but she grinned anyway. "It comes with the job. Besides, isn't that like the pot calling the kettle black?"

Lance smiled. She had him there. "Why fund-raising?"

"Oh, no you don't." She laughed. "Why turtles?"

The tips of her hair brushed against his fingers; he fought the urge to plunge them into it. "I already told you."

"But I didn't believe you."

This time when her hair grazed his skin, he caught the silky strands and rubbed them between his fingers. He immediately knew his mistake. One touch would never be enough.

"The other night," he murmured, his voice thick, "when I took a walk on the beach, I got so damn angry. A half a dozen homes had spotlights shining on the beach. Lights on the beach confuse the turtles, inhibit them from nesting, and lead to the deaths of hundreds of hatchlings. We fought to get a city ordinance passed prohibiting lights on the beach. Now the problem is getting people to comply."

"Do you get a lot of that?"

"Stupidity? Yes, we do." His jaw tightened. "We've come upon adults trying to ride a mama turtle as she made her way up the beach. It's just so damn . . ."

He shook his head as if to shake off his frustration, and Madi experienced again that funny little pinch in her chest, somewhere in the vicinity of her heart. Even as she blamed the seafood canapés she'd sampled each time a waiter had passed with a tray, she acknowledged the truth. This man was more than he seemed, more than she'd first judged him to be. And that scared the hell out of her.

Even though she knew she should cut and run, she lifted her gaze to his and smiled. "I got into fund-raising both by accident and quite naturally, if that makes sense. My mother's hopelessly scatterbrained, but loves being the social queen bee. She'd make all sorts of outrageous commitments to charities—to host raffles and luncheon benefits and even black tie extravaganzas. Of course, she was always in way over her head.

"Even when I was a child, I saw that. I knew I had to help. In the process I discovered I was a whiz at organization and that my taste was impeccable, whether I was planning a Southern-style barbecue or a black tie gala. After a while, the charities approached me instead of my mother.

One finally offered me a job." She angled him a glance. "Satisfied?"

He wasn't. Not nearly. None of that told him why he hadn't been able to take his eyes off her all night. Why he couldn't still. "And that's it?"

Her mouth curved in a teasing smile. "Well, I suppose there's one more little thing."

"And that is?"

"People like to give me money—lots and lots of money." He didn't laugh as she'd expected him to. Instead he drew his eyebrows together and studied her with the intensity of a scientist examining a new form of life. She cleared her throat. "Lance, I'm starting to feel like a bug in a glass. Mind sharing your thoughts?"

"You're one of the sexiest women I've ever met."

The compliment sounded not like a compliment at all. In fact, the words seemed almost grudging. She laughed. "Well, thank you."

"I'm not telling you anything you haven't heard a hundred times before. We both know that."

"True, but your delivery was . . . completely unique."

He smiled. "You're also self-confident to the point of being cocky, and by all indications a capable, even hard-nosed, professional."

He shook his head and his hair tumbled across his forehead. Madi caught herself a moment before she reached up to push it back. Instead she flattened her hands against his chest. "So? Is there anything wrong with being those things?"

"Not at all. I guess I'm more interested in your secrets." He tightened his fingers at her waist. "Have you any, Madi Muldoon?"

"We all have secrets," she murmured. "You have them."

"Do I?"

"Mmm." She smoothed her fingers over his fine worsted jacket until she reached the crisp cotton of his shirt. "I just don't know what they are . . . yet."

"There's that self-confidence again."

"I can't help myself."

He laughed and swung her around, and as he did, her thigh brushed his. Arousal sliced through him, catching him off-guard. His smile faded and he gazed down at her beautiful, amused face. He wanted to kiss her, wanted to capture that lovely mobile mouth and taste her laughter, her life.

But to do so would be to break promises he'd made to himself long ago, to forget plans already set in motion.

He dragged his gaze back to hers. "Does that confidence ever flag, Madi Muldoon? Are there any chinks in your armor, or are you as invulnerable as you seem?"

At his softly spoken words, the image of her niece's sweet, innocent face popped into her head. And with the image came an ache that was gentle, persistent, and absolutely debilitating.

Lance heard her sharply drawn breath, saw the emotions that passed lightning fast across her features. The words he'd spoken so glibly, so carelessly, had hurt her. He felt regret and a moment of blind terror. This seemingly unscathable woman had a place that was soft and too touchable.

Madi tipped her chin up, furious with him for the question, but more furious with herself for the self-doubt. She worked to keep her voice light, even. "And is there anything about you that's warm or emotional or spontaneous? Or are you simply what you appear—the businessman driven to success at all costs?"

Lance told himself it was to prove a point. He told himself it had nothing to do with soft, secret places or barely veiled vulnerabilities and everything to do with being in control.

He lowered his mouth until it hovered only a whisper from hers. He caught the fresh scent of her shampoo, the sultry one of her perfume; he saw that her eyes weren't brown at all, but tawny— like a cat's. In them he read shock . . . and arousal.

Lifting his hands, he tangled his fingers in her wild mane of hair. He'd wanted to do that since the first morning he'd seen the wind toss it. He wasn't disappointed—the strands felt luxurious, even exotic, against his fingers. He knew they would feel even more so against other, more sensitive parts of his anatomy.

He caught his breath, thoughts of plans and promises and control evaporating. He lowered his mouth even more . . . but still didn't kiss her.

Madi curled her fingers around his shoulders. He hardly touched her, yet she felt as if he touched her everywhere. Parts of her body she'd not been aware of before tingled—the backs of her knees, the nape of her neck, the insides of her elbows. And the places of which she had already been aware . . . those places were aflame. It was as if all of her trembled in anticipation of his kiss.

She swayed toward him in silent invitation. His

breath stirred against her mouth and she parted her lips.

A moment later he dropped his hands and stepped away.

For one split second, she was dizzy with denial and desire. Then reality—and anger—crept over her. He'd surprised her this time. He wouldn't again.

She met his gaze evenly. "I told you before, Lance Alexander, you can't intimidate me."

Lance studied her flushed face, regret warring with reason. "And I told you, I wouldn't try."

Madi assured herself that what she felt was fury, yet the trembling in her knees told her otherwise. She promised herself she was totally unaffected and totally in control. Her runaway pulse contradicted her. She worked to disguise her telltale, ragged breathing. "Right. Tell me another one."

"Okay, Hollywood." He took a step toward her, lowering his voice to a husky whisper. "I think you wanted me to kiss you. I think you wanted that . . . badly."

"Poor man, you're delusional." He only smiled, and she silently swore. "Let's set some ground rules here. We're colleagues, nothing more. I don't get involved with people I work with, not ever."

"Who's getting involved? I was merely proving a point."

"A point?" She tossed her hair over her shoulder; the wind tossed it back.

"You asked if there was anything warm or spontaneous about me. I could have been more spontaneous and a hell of a lot warmer, but I thought that would suffice."

Heat stung her cheeks, and she cursed the revealing color. She'd been bested. Totally, un-equivocably. She wouldn't allow it to happen again. She smiled coolly. "If one needs to be prompted to spontaneous acts, I hardly think a point's been proved. If you'll excuse me, there are wallets waiting to be picked."

He laughed. "I'll see you Monday morning at the Sea Turtle Society. Is nine all right?"

"Fine."

"It's a date, then."

She caught herself a moment before she spun around and corrected him. Instead she murmured, "It's a date."

Three

Monday morning arrived too quickly. Madi pulled
to a stop in front of the Sea Turtle Society's offices,
but didn't immediately get out of her car. In a few
moments she would have to face Lance again, face
him and pretend she hadn't thought about him all
weekend, pretend she hadn't stewed and ranted
and ached over his not kissing her—and her wanting him to so badly.

Ridiculous! She opened the car door, stepped
out, then snapped it shut behind her. She was
annoyed he'd outsmarted her. No one did that,
especially a man whose idea of fun was the financial page and a cup of decaf.

Madi flipped her hair over her shoulder. And she
certainly hadn't been bothered by the fact he'd hit
on a dozen different women that night, but when
he'd approached her all he'd wanted to do was
"prove a point." She preferred it that way.

Sure she did.

Madi drew in another deep, steadying breath. She had herself in control now. She would do what she did best—flirt, tease, keep things light and superficial. He wouldn't get under her skin again.

And maybe in the bargain, she'd get one up on him.

Satisfied, she started up the walk leading to the S.T.S. offices. Located on the oldest street in Melbourne Beach, the dilapidated building appeared to have once been a summer cottage.

Madi frowned as she stepped onto the porch and crossed to the door. She'd known she was scaling down when she took this assignment, she just hadn't realized how much.

Unbelievably, the interior of the Society was more unassuming than the exterior. A single information counter occupied one wall, an old loveseat another. Unorganized stacks of literature littered the counter—presumably containing information about the turtles.

Madi walked into the room. "Anybody home?" she called.

From a door to her right appeared a very pregnant young woman. She smiled warmly. "You must be Madi."

"I am." Madi returned her smile and stepped farther into the room. "And you are . . . ?"

"Jenny." She held out her hand. "I'm the Monday, Wednesday, and Friday morning volunteer."

"Nice to meet you, Jenny." Madi smiled again, hiding her dismay. The last charity she'd worked for had had professional office space and three full-time employees. "I believe I'm supposed to meet Mr. Alexander here this morning."

Jenny's cheeks pinkened and she placed her hands on her swollen belly. "He called. He's running late and asked that you wait."

Madi narrowed her eyes. "Did he happen to mention why he was running late or how long he might be?" She asked even though she understood his game. This was another of his intimidation techniques.

"No, but he told me to collect some information for you." The young woman crossed to the counter and picked up a bulging manila envelope. As she did she made a small sound of discomfort. "Sorry, I'm eight months now, and my back's killing me."

"My sister just had a baby. A little girl." Madi realized she was staring at the young woman's stomach and, disconcerted, lifted her gaze back to her face. "Her back hurt a lot too."

"I'm hoping for a girl, but Rick, that's my husband, he wants a boy. We'll be happy with whatever we get." She laughed giddily. "What did they name her?"

Madi swallowed past the lump that had lodged in her throat. "Morgan."

Jenny wrinkled her nose. "I like the old-fashioned girl-names better—like Emily or Elizabeth. Do you have any children, Madi?"

"No." She cleared her throat. "I'm really not a 'children' person."

"Really? I would have thought by the way you—"

"No," Madi repeated, holding out her hand for the envelope. She swore silently as the hand trembled. "I better get started on that. If you could point me in the direction of my office?"

The word office, Madi thought a minute later as she looked around the tiny cubicle, was being used rather loosely. In fact, she suspected this space had been a closet until a week ago, and if she investigated she would find Lance at the bottom of its selection.

Straightening her spine, she swung around and marched back out front. Lance Alexander would not have the last word, not this time. "Jenny, does Mr. Alexander keep an office here at the Society?"

"Jenny looked up from a baby book by Dr. Spock. "Yes. Although he really doesn't use it much."

"Is this it?" She indicated the door Jenny had come out of earlier. The young woman nodded and Madi stuck her head inside. The room was large and light and airy. Even with several full-sized filing cabinets and an oversized desk, there was plenty of space.

Jenny walked up beside her. "Your office is a little small, isn't it?"

"Little and small being the operative words," Madi muttered, then turned back to the volunteer. "Mr. Alexander and I will be sharing this space for the time being. When he comes in, be sure to direct him to me."

Two hours later Madi looked up as the office door swung open. Today his suit was gray with the subtlest of stripes. It fit snugly over his shoulders, tapering down to his lean hips. Her heart did an annoying little sidestep. She scowled and glanced pointedly at her watch. "Lance, how nice of you to stop by."

"I apologize for my tardiness."

No explanation. No pleas for forgiveness. She arched an eyebrow and flipped shut the file she'd been studying. "Nice office. Wish I could say the same about mine."

He shut the door behind him, then leaned against it, obviously amused. "Jenny tells me you weren't impressed with the one I arranged for you."

Her annoyance grew. "Jenny has a gift for understatement."

"She also told me you'd commandeered mine."

With a satisfied smile, Madi leaned back in her/his chair. "I hope you don't mind."

He laughed and crossed to the desk. "Not at all. This way it'll be much easier to keep an eye on you." He lowered himself into the chair across from her. "I don't have a lot of time, so why don't we begin."

Madi gritted her teeth. Despite her best intentions about remaining businesslike, the man had to do no more than look at her, and the desire to kiss him swelled within her once more. Dammit.

"I've been going over the Society's financial records," she said, managing to keep her voice cool. "You're not doing much better than keeping your heads above water."

"Pardon the pun."

She lifted her brows at the joke, openly studying him. His disconcerting green eyes were crinkled at the corners, and his finely cut mouth turned up in the smallest of smiles. He looked amused, relaxed, and sexy as hell. Something must be up. "I can see why the board was desperate to acquire my services. You need the help of a professional."

"What I don't need, Hollywood, is a sell job. You've been hired. Nothing you can say will change my mind about which way I voted."

"No?" She brazenly trailed her gaze over him. "Maybe this will have some effect. I will, at a minimum, triple what you've collected in your best year."

He returned her gaze, just as brazenly. "Before or after your salary?"

"After. Easily." She stood and crossed to one of the large windows. Outside a mother herded her two children away from the street. Madi turned her back on the scene and faced Lance once more. "You've been missing the boat. Individual and corporate donations are fine, but the big money is brought into charities with fund-raising events."

"Like golf tournaments?"

"Exactly. Golfers tend to be obsessive about their sport. The idea of getting to play *and* using the fee as a tax deduction, well, it doesn't get any better than that." She perched on the edge of the desk. "The truth is, for most people, knowing they're saving the turtles or helping find a cure for cancer isn't enough. They want to have fun while they're doing it."

Lance leaned forward and lightly touched the wooden bangle bracelet on her wrist. His flesh didn't meet hers. The gesture would no doubt have been considered totally benign by an onlooker.

Madi almost laughed out loud. *Benign*? That one small gesture had the blood careening through her veins and her head emptying of everything even remotely sensible.

He lifted his gaze from the bracelet to her face. Her breath caught. She'd thought she would read confidence, even satisfaction in his eyes. Instead she saw questions . . . questions and something else, something that had her thinking of shared secrets and long, hot afternoons spent together in a darkened bedroom.

A second later all she saw was the determination of a man accustomed to winning. She shook her head and wondered if she'd imagined the other.

"Isn't all this 'fun' a little iffy?" he asked softly. "Doesn't the success of the event depend on how many people attend?"

It took her a moment to drag her thoughts back to their conversation, and she cursed the small sign of vulnerability. "Sure," she said. "But that's where I come in. Everything will be meticulously planned, carefully targeted. Items needed to throw the various bashes are donated—country clubs, liquor, even advertising. All participating businesses get their names out there in front of the public and a tax deduction."

"*Much* is donated," he corrected her, "not all."

She bit back a sound of frustration. "That's another place the ability of the fund-raiser makes a difference. I'll be able to get twice as much donated as one of your volunteers."

"But the price tag for one of these parties can

still be pretty steep. The Society could go in the hole."

This time she made no effort to hold back her frustration. "The possibility is there. Fund-raising contains an element of risk. But like any investment, the rewards can be stupendous. The board checked me out. I've never lost money for an organization. In fact, I've never done anything but made money. You're not taking much of a risk with me."

He met her gaze, seemingly unaffected—or unimpressed—by everything she'd said. "What's next?"

"Next I plan our calendar of events, then I'll begin finding volunteers and corporate sponsors."

"I want to be included every step of the way." He got to his feet. "And I want to see all arrangements before you present them to the board."

Madi stood, too, narrowing her eyes. She could refuse; she would be within her rights. She preferred another tack. "Going through the files I found some interesting clippings." She sent him her most winning smile. "It seems your association with the Society has been lucrative—P.R.- wise, that is."

She thumbed through the file and pulled out half a dozen newspaper and magazine articles. In all Lance was prominently featured. "Enlightened self-interest is a wonderful thing—giving something for something in return. That's what our sponsors and patrons do. In a way it's what I do. Everybody wins by my thinking." She nudged the articles toward him with her forefinger.

"What are you saying?"

She shrugged. "It doesn't hurt to be a developer associated with an environmental concern. Makes for good press, don't you think?"

He stiffened. "You're determined to think I'm a coldhearted entrepreneur who rapes the land and uses the turtles as a way to convince the public otherwise."

She'd offended him. She saw it in his eyes, in the muscle that twitched in his jaw. The other night, when they'd danced, she'd foolishly believed what he'd said about the turtles, about his altruistic intentions. And in doing so, she'd lowered her guard.

"I've been in this business a long time," she said quietly. "Few people's characters are sterling, almost never are their reasons for helping selfless. I don't think any less of you. This is the way it's done."

For a full ten seconds he stared at her, his expression stony. When he spoke, his voice was low and tight. "It's easier for you this way, isn't it? Keep me in the tidy little box you've fashioned for me and everybody's safe. Especially you."

Her stomach crashed to her knees. "Nonsense."

He took a step closer to her. "Is it?"

She fought the urge to back up. "Yes."

"Think you're up to a late night tonight?"

She arched an eyebrow at his change of subject. "Depends on what you have in mind."

"Turtle patrol. It's about time you saw the real thing. I'll arrange the use of a couple of the Society's three-wheelers and we'll comb the beach until we find one. Who knows, maybe you'll even get lucky."

He started for the door. She stopped him. "Lucky, Lance?"

"Yeah." He looked back over his shoulder at her. "Maybe you'll see several. See you tonight, Hollywood."

Seven hours later, Lance tossed down his pencil and swore. He'd read the same figures half a dozen times and still had no idea what they were.

Madison Muldoon was driving him crazy.

He pressed the heels of his hands to his eyes. He couldn't stop thinking about her. Every time he saw her he told himself he would figure out why she fascinated him so, but each time, instead of answers, he got more questions . . . and he became more intrigued.

He picked up his pencil once again, but only tapped it on the financial report. It shouldn't matter that she thought he was an ambitious bastard who used charitywork for free publicity. It shouldn't matter, and he told himself it didn't.

But if that was the case, why had he offered to take her on turtle patrol that night? And why did it feel like he'd taken a good right hook to the gut?

Dammit, she'd gotten under his skin.

"Hi, neighbor. Still working I see."

He looked up to Madi's third-story deck. She smiled sleepily down at him, and all those places that already ached tightened a bit more. Her hair fell in a glorious tumble around her face; she wore an oversized T-shirt that said something about cowboys and saddles. He knew he'd be dreaming that night about what was under the shirt. "Yes," he replied. "Still working."

"What time is it?" She yawned and stretched. The T-shirt inched up her thighs.

Lance followed the path of the fabric, his mouth suddenly dry. "Seven-thirty-three."

"That late already?" She leaned on the railing. "What's on the grill?"

He tossed his pencil on top of the papers once more. "Chicken."

"And the wine?" She motioned to the glass beside him.

"Chardonnay."

She grinned. "I love chicken."

So that was it. He smiled, enjoying her boldness. "Is that so?"

Madi rested her elbows on her weathered wood railing and propped her chin on her fist. "Mmm . . . especially the drumsticks."

"You don't say?"

"Uh-huh." She cocked her head to one side. "You know, we never discussed what time we were meeting."

"True."

"And as long as we're getting together later . . ."

"Yes?"

"And I haven't found time to stock my cupboards or fridge . . ."

"Why doesn't that surprise me?"

"We could get together now."

Lance bit back a smile. "There's no sense in that. The turtles don't nest until late."

She scowled. "Okay, Alexander, here's the deal.

I'll give you five bucks for a few scraps of food and more if you throw in a glass of wine."

He laughed. "You're really something, you know that?"

"Okay." She pushed the hair away from her face. "Six-fifty, but I don't think you're being very neighborly."

"Six-fifty?"

"And not a penny more."

"I can't take money from you."

"Really?"

She was the picture of innocence, and he laughed again. "I'll say this for you, Madison Muldoon, you're damn good at wangling free meals."

"Some might even call me a professional." She started back inside, then stopped and looked coquettishly over her shoulder at him. "Do I have time to wash my face?"

"By all means." He shook his head, watching as she disappeared through her sliding glass doors. Why did she have to be so damn gorgeous? Couldn't she have a wart or a mole or . . .

He didn't finish the thought. What made Madi Muldoon so attractive, so special, had little to do with looks and more to do with something less obvious, something that kept eluding him.

He'd told her he didn't like mysteries. And he didn't. He liked logic and closure and control. None of those things applied to Madi. Not yet, anyway.

He smiled and crossed to the grill. But they would. Narrowing his eyes in determination, he attended to the chicken.

Fifteen minutes later Madi walked from her patio to Lance's. Although she hadn't bothered with makeup, she had taken the time to run a comb through her hair and change her clothes. She'd chosen a peacock-blue tank top and matching shorts for comfort. The evening was nearly as warm as the afternoon had been.

She drew in a deep breath when she saw he was waiting for her. This time, she promised herself, smiling in greeting, she would keep it light and teasing. She would be in control.

Then he handed her a glass of wine. Their fingers met; her pulse scrambled. This wouldn't do, she thought, not at all. She'd better pull herself together and fast, or soon she would be pulling herself out of deep trouble.

Ignoring the curious little flutters and tiny annoying tingles, she smiled again. "I hope I haven't held you up?"

"Not at all. The chicken still has about twenty minutes to go." He motioned to the wrought-iron patio set. "Have a seat while I get a few things together."

She sank into one of the sling-style chairs. "Can I help?"

"Are you any good in the kitchen?"

"I'm great at organizing others, but on my own I'm nothing but trouble."

He eyed her speculatively, then nodded. "With a capital T, no doubt. Stay put, I can do without that this week."

For several minutes she watched as he moved around the patio, checking the grill, skewering vegetables for shish kabobs, pausing to sip his wine. His movements were clean and efficient. He was, she realized, a man accustomed to taking care of himself, a man comfortable with his life, his world. And for some reason she found those qualities endearing.

Endearing? She scowled and swallowed some of the crisp, dry wine. Ridiculous! She found his type of man irritating.

Even so, the funniest twinge settled in the pit of her stomach. The sensation, she knew, had nothing to do with hunger and everything to do with . . . what? Not nerves, certainly not insecurity. She'd learned to control both of those years ago.

And it couldn't be awareness.

She caught her bottom lip between her teeth. No, not awareness. She didn't know Lance Alexander very well, but she knew enough to see he wasn't for her. Life had taught her many lessons, and the biggest had been about men like Lance Alexander.

"Is there something wrong with the wine?"

She jerked her head up at Lance's question. "I'm sorry, what?"

"The wine? You were glaring at it."

"Was I?" Her laugh sounded forced even to her own ears. "It's great, delicious."

"Good. We're about ready, so pour yourself another glass and take a plate."

Forty-five minutes later, they both pushed their plates away. "Wonderful," Madi murmured, sighing and leaning back in her chair. "I haven't had a meal like that in a long time."

"You must eat out a lot."

"Too much." She smiled unselfconsciously. "But then, considering my kitchen abilities, maybe it's better that way."

Lance twirled his empty wineglass between his fingers. Madi watched the movement of those strong, tanned fingers against the delicate crystal, and wondered what they would feel like against other, even more delicate things. Realizing her thoughts, she glanced at her own half-empty glass. It was time to switch to water. The wine had started to affect her judgment.

"Tell me about your mother, Madi."

"My mother?" she repeated, surprised. Through dinner they'd kept up a constant but impersonal conversation. He'd told her the history of Melbourne Beach; she'd shared some amusing anecdotes from past fund-raising events. Now, even his tone seemed changed. Huskier, more intimate. "What brought this on?"

He shrugged and refilled her wineglass. "You talked about her the other evening, and now I'm curious. I got the feeling she's both scatterbrained and softhearted."

"Actually, that describes her very well."

"So she's the traditional cookie-baking mom with silvering hair and a flour-dusted apron?"

Madi pictured her beautiful social butterfly of a mother and laughed. "Not quite. My mother's an actress."

"Would I know her work?"

"Not unless your taste in celluloid runs to things like *Godzilla Returns* and *Beach Blanket Birthday Party*."

"Your mother's a B-movie star?"

Madi grinned at the incredulity in his voice. "B-minus, and the word 'star' is questionable. Most of her roles have been bits or extras." She leaned her head back and looked up at the darkening sky. "But what Delilah's missing in talent, she makes up for in looks."

"You've inherited her beauty."

At his murmured compliment, one of those annoying tingles eased up her spine. Madi blamed the soft sea breeze. "No. As Delilah says, I inherited the curse of the Muldoons—overbearing bone structure."

Lance chuckled. "What's he like?"

"Patrick Muldoon?" She squinted up at the heavens, then glanced back at him. "Truthfully, I don't know. He was an extremely successful businessman and didn't have a lot of time for little girls with runny noses and big dreams. I haven't seen him in almost fifteen years."

"I'm sorry."

"Don't be." The catch in her voice surprised her. She swallowed and tried again. "It stopped hurting a long time ago."

Silence fell between them. It seemed to Madi to be at once awkward and comforting. After a moment, Lance cleared his throat. "My mother never married."

Madi stared at him. She saw by his expression he was just as shocked as she by his admission. She also saw more than a trace of pain. "Never?"

"Never," he repeated. "She could have, once. A man, a nice man, wanted her to . . . wanted us to be a family. But she said no."

Madi's voice was husky as she spoke around the lump that had settled in her throat. "What happened?"

"She didn't love him enough, or not the right

way." Lance gazed out at the water. "At least that's what she said."

Warmth and regret ballooned inside her. She ached for him, for this man she hardly knew and dared not trust. "It must have been tough for you," she murmured. "How did you make it?"

"We both worked hard—she worked too hard." He frowned at the ocean. "She had a day job and did cleaning at night."

It didn't escape Madi that he spoke of them when she'd been speaking only of him. She reached across the table and caught his hand.

He dragged his gaze back to hers, and she saw the sadness shadowing his eyes. "My mother believed in Cinderella stories and knights in shining armor. She never gave up the ridiculous hope that my father would come for her. She was a hopeless romantic until the day she died."

Madi slipped her hand from his, a trembling sensation in the pit of her stomach. Why did there have to be another side to this man? A gentle, vulnerable side? Why couldn't he be just what he seemed—hard and determined and unforgiving? "At least," she said lightly, "you didn't have to endure the constant arguing. Thank heaven mine finally divorced. Of course, then there was husband number two. I'm not sure if he was worse, or if time and distance made my father look good."

Lance's expression cleared. "How old were you when they divorced?"

"Six."

"Do you have any siblings?"

"One, by Delilah's third husband. Tina's the best."

Lance arched his brows. "Just how many husbands has your mother had?"

Madi laughed. "My mother never said no to a proposal. She's on number six or seven now. I lose track."

"How do you feel about that?"

Madi paused. Odd how he questioned her, she mused, as if he were part reporter, part shrink. She shook off the sensation. "I'm not angry, if that's what you're getting at. She's a wonderful person but has the same problem a lot of women have when it comes to men and love—an inability to make wise choices."

"Sounds like a tough childhood." He began to twirl his wineglass again. "You know, they say the first five years of a child's life are the most important."

"Do they?" She gazed curiously at him. "This doesn't seem like your type of subject matter."

"I've been doing a little research," he returned easily. "How do you feel about day-care?"

She knew for a fact he'd been doing research. This song and dance had a familiar ring. "I haven't thought about it much. Why do you ask?"

"Just curious. More wine?" He lifted the bottle, then set it back down when she shook her head. "What about the future, Madi? Do you plan to keep traveling or are you going to settle down and—"

"Would you like me to get you a pen and piece of paper?"

"What do you mean?"

"I mean, it must be hard to keep the answers of so many different women straight." She gave him an amused glance. "I overheard some of your conversations at the party the other night. What's going on, Lance? What am I being tested for—the woman who will be the mother of your children?"

He met her gaze, his own serious. "Something like that."

Her amusement evaporated. It was replaced by astonishment. "Wait a minute. You're saying you want to marry me?"

"Not exactly." He cleared his throat. "I'm ready to get married. I've built a successful business. Now I want a family."

It took her a full ten seconds to pull herself together. When she had, she arched her eyebrows coolly. "So, you're shopping for a wife?"

Lance pushed away from the table and stood. Crossing to the edge of the patio, he looked out at the ocean. In that moment, oddly, he thought of his mother and being a boy again. Maybe because he was getting so close to bringing the last of his dreams to fruition.

He drew a deep breath and turned back to her. "I could waste months, years even, randomly dating women, starting and ending relationships. I turn forty this year, Madi. I don't have that kind of time to waste."

"So you decided to speed up the process."

"Exactly. I devised a list of questions ranging from ideas about child rearing to religious beliefs. The questions reflect my own beliefs and what I determined most important to a lasting marriage. I date the women whose answers mesh with mine. Those whose don't, I don't. It seemed a more expedient approach to—"

"Expedient," she repeated, unable to hold her

tongue one more second. "You devised 'a plan' to find a wife? Do you really believe you can find love the same way you find a new secretar—"

"No." Lance pushed at the hair that tumbled across his forehead. "I'm not looking for love, I'm looking for a mate, a partner. I want a strong marriage, a marriage that will last 'until death do us part.' That kind of marriage is based on mutual respect and shared goals, not on some figment of the imagination called love."

"I don't believe this," Madi muttered, even as she told herself Lance Alexander was nothing to her but a colleague, told herself it shouldn't matter.

But it did matter. And the truth of that infuriated her all the more.

"You are the most calculating, manipulative man I have ever met and believe me, I've met some doozies. And if I were going to get married—which I am not ever going to do—a man who would choose his wife with all the emotion of a catalogue shopper would be the last man I'd ever consider."

"What's wrong with logic?" he asked, feeling her words like a punch to his midsection. "What's wrong with using your head instead of your heart—or other parts of the anatomy—when choosing a mate? It's rewarded in all other areas of—"

"Because it's not real. It's not warm . . . it's not human. We are creatures who need to love and be loved. It's the best of what we are."

"I disagree. We are self-destructive creatures who act foolishly out of passion."

She forced herself to stay seated, to keep a

semblance of control. "Mergers are for corporations."

"Company mergers last far longer than most marriages. Take your own mother for—"

"Leave my mother out of this!"

"Fine." He glared at her, angry at his own need to defend himself, to convince her. But as he did, something changed. He became aware of the way she held herself, full of emotion and the strength of her own conviction. He became aware of her eyes snapping with righteous indignation, of the wild color in her cheeks. And he became aware of one other thing—this was a different Madi from the one she normally presented to the world. Gone was the flirt, the insouciant tease. Here was a woman of great emotion, of deeply felt beliefs.

Lance sucked in a sharp breath. This was the Madi he'd glimpsed before. And she was a hundred times more exciting, a thousand times more appealing than the other. It was a shame she was the wrong woman for him.

"Don't worry," he said softly, deliberately. "I'm not going to try to coerce you into marrying me. You flunked the test anyway."

"What!"

He smiled at the outrage in that one word. Drawing her emotions to the surface could become addictive. "I knew all along you were wrong for the job, but I thought I'd give you a try anyway."

"Give me a try!" Madi wanted to hit him. Breathing deeply, she reined in her anger. She'd promised herself she would not let him get to her, and here she was fighting mad. What did it matter to her if he wanted to select a wife with all the heart of choosing a brand of bologna? It didn't. And so what if he thought love was a foolish figment of the imagination? She couldn't care less.

Then why was her heart thundering in her chest? Why were her palms damp, her cheeks hot?

Outrage, she told herself. Yes, that was it. She might even be able to have a little fun with this "find a wife thing."

She took a calming breath, then another. "I'm glad we got that out of the way now, Lance," she said finally, putting just the right amount of amusement and sincerity into her voice.

He realized he was staring at her too-tempting mouth and jerked his gaze away. "Are you?"

"Why, yes." She sent him her best and most brilliant smile. "This way no silly little thing like a marriage proposal will get in the way of our fund-raising project."

Lance cocked an eyebrow. Where was the woman of heat, the one who had faced him in outrage a moment ago? Regret curled through him, followed by relief. It was just as well, he told himself. That woman had been far too tempting. "Just because our beliefs are different doesn't mean we can't work together."

"Exactly."

"So, despite my manipulative, Neanderthal ways, you still want to go on turtle patrol?"

"Absolutely. But I believe my description was manipulative, calculating, and totally devoid of human warmth."

"Thanks for refreshing my memory. If you're ready?"

He smiled at her then. The curving of his lips

was totally masculine and, somehow, totally in control. Madi silently swore as she followed him across the lawn and toward the boardwalk. If nothing else, this evening had shown her exactly what type of man Lance Alexander was.

She'd let her guard slip, momentarily. She wouldn't again.

Four

There were two three-wheelers waiting for them at the end of the boardwalk. "Ever ride one of these before?" Lance asked.

Madi shook her head. "But I won't have a problem."

"Great." He tossed her a key. "We'll look for a couple of hours. If we haven't spotted one by then we can stop and reevaluate. Okay?"

She nodded. After he told her to stay close and go slow, they took off. The beach was completely dark, and save for the sound of the ocean and their bikes, totally quiet. Madi rode a little behind Lance, following his signals to slow down or turn toward or away from the dune.

When an hour had passed with no sign of a turtle, she started to feel discouraged. Just then Lance waved her to a stop. One of the huge creatures was making its way up the beach toward the dune.

At first all Madi could make out was a large, low

shape, then as she and Lance dismounted the bikes and crept closer, her eyes adjusted to the dark and she saw what so many people were working so hard to save.

Her breath caught. Nothing could have prepared her for the sight before her—not all the reading she'd done, not the illustrations and pictures she'd seen. The turtle was much larger than she'd thought it would be. She'd read all the facts, that loggerheads—the most common type of turtle to nest in Florida—could reach thirty-eight inches long and three hundred and fifty pounds; that they were prehistoric creatures, having roamed the sea for millions of years; and that the nesting process was an arduous one for the female. But reading facts couldn't compare with witnessing them. Not by a long shot.

"She's easily spooked at this stage," Lance whispered. "Once she begins digging her nest she goes into a trance of sorts, but until then any noise or light can startle her and send her back to the water."

Madi nodded even though she knew he wasn't looking at her. He, like she, couldn't take his eyes off the sea turtle. There was something both touching and inspiring about the way the female moved gracelessly—lumbered really—toward the dune.

And magical. Madi swallowed past the lump in her throat. She was witnessing something that had nothing to do with being a human but everything to do with being alive.

She stepped closer to Lance and took his hand, wanting without words to communicate her wonder to him. He curled his fingers around hers and squeezed, and she knew she didn't have to. He understood. He felt the same.

Several times during her trip up the beach, the mama turtle stopped and dug into the sand with her snout. Each time Madi held her breath, afraid the creature would change her mind, turn around and go back.

"What's she doing?" she asked Lance, keeping her voice low.

"Testing the sand," he answered. "Although we're not sure exactly for what. Maybe temperature, maybe water content or even smell."

Finally the turtle found a satisfactory place very near the dune and began, as Lance told her, making a body pit. Madi watched as the turtle, using her limbs and rotating her body, excavated the sand until she had created a dishlike indentation that was at least ten feet across.

"We can talk now," Lance murmured, moving nearer the turtle and indicating that Madi should follow.

Madi didn't want to talk, and judging by Lance's silence, neither did he. She followed him cautiously, still afraid the female would abandon her task and head for the ocean. She didn't, though, and Madi saw what Lance had meant by "trance of sorts." The creature was completely oblivious to their presence.

Madi sank to the ground. The air had cooled, but the breeze off the ocean was still mild. Slipping off her sandals, she dug her toes into the warm sand.

The turtle continued to work. Sand flew as she raked her powerful flippers over it. Then, using her back flippers, she began to dig the actual cavity for the eggs. One hind flipper scooped, the other smoothed the discarded sand to the side.

"She's beautiful, isn't she?" Lance said, tenderly

smoothing the sand off the turtle's back, checking her over.

Madi watched him, her chest tight with emotion. That morning she had accused him of enlightened self-interest. She saw now that it was so much more than that. He really cared about these creatures.

"Dammit." He drew his eyebrows together as he found a deep gash in the turtle's shell.

Madi leaned closer, concerned. "What caused that?"

"It could have been fishing lines, but more likely it was a power boat propeller. They do unbelievable damage to the turtles and manatees."

She shifted her gaze from Lance to the nesting turtle. "Poor old girl."

"She's still alive," Lance said grimly. "She's still producing eggs." He squatted down, caught one of the eggs, and held it out to her. It was smooth, white, and about the size of a Ping-Pong ball. "She'll lay up to one hundred and twenty eggs per clutch and from one to nine clutches over the season."

Madi touched it. It was covered with a thin, clear fluid. "This won't hurt it?"

"No. Once the eggs are in the nest they can't be disturbed, but it's fine now as long as you're careful."

She touched the egg again. "How many make it?"

"Not enough. Some of the eggs are yolkless and don't hatch, many nests are washed or eroded away, eggs are taken by raccoons and other natural predators." He paused. "And many nests are picked clean."

Madi frowned. "Picked clean?"

"Turtle eggs are a delicacy. Whole nesting

beaches have been wiped out by egg hunters. Here in the United States nests are protected, but worldwide it's a problem of epidemic proportions."

"But if the eggs continue to be taken how will the turtles . . ." She didn't finish the question. They both knew the answer already. The species wouldn't survive.

She turned back to the turtle, then gasped in surprise. "She's crying." Blinking against the moisture in her own eyes, she looked at Lance. "Are they tears of relief or joy? Or does she weep at the plight of her species?"

"Nothing nearly so romantic," he said dryly. "While they lay, tears stream from their eyes. The moisture keeps their eyes from drying out and protects them from sand and other grit."

Lance's words were clipped, his explanation factual, unemotional. But something in his eyes answered her differently. Something in their depths spoke of endless emotion. She felt a tug, a pull, and called herself a fool.

The female had finished laying and began covering her nest much in the same way she'd dug it. That done, she turned and started back to the ocean. Madi saw the turtle's exhaustion in the way she moved, could feel it somewhere inside of herself, in a part that was as ancient as this act had been.

They followed. Once again Madi slipped her hand into Lance's. And once again he twined his fingers with hers.

When the first wave rushing onto the shore reached the turtle, a feeling of intense relief and joy swept over Madi. She clutched Lance's hand as another wave almost took the turtle, then laughed out loud as one finally did. A second later the turtle disappeared into the black, endless ocean.

Madi turned her face to Lance's, another laugh bubbling to her lips. As their eyes met, her laughter died. She brought her hands to his chest, he brought his to her hair. For long moments they stared at each other, then he lowered his mouth to hers.

In that moment Madi didn't know if her heart completely stopped, or if it started for the first time. All she knew was an ache deep in her chest, emboldening and wondrous.

She gave into the ache and let sensation rush over her, much as the water had rushed over the turtle moments ago. She gave into it, let it swallow and surround her, and instead of feeling suffocated, she experienced a curious sense of being grounded, connected.

His lips were firm and warm and strong against hers. His earthy scent, a combination of clean air and salt water and things that thrived on both, filled her head. Or was it the scent of the beach? It made no difference. He was as much a part of this place, this experience, as the sea turtle had been.

He was as definable . . . and as much of a mystery.

She curled her hands into the soft cotton of his T-shirt. Underneath her fingers his heart beat strong but not quite steadily, and she smiled a little. This man, with all his logic, was as affected by her as she by him.

Lance tore his lips from hers, then trailed his across her smooth cheek until he found the fragrant flesh of her neck. He discovered the place right below her ear where her pulse beat wildly. Her scent—at once sweet and exotic—was most potent there, and he drew it, her, in. He couldn't get enough. It was as if he'd never smelled, tasted, or touched a woman before.

He'd expected surprise, even regret in her response. Instead she tasted of acceptance and invitation. He'd thought her kiss would be skilled, even facile. Instead she seemed almost youthful and unpracticed.

He knew she wasn't for him. He'd hoped, with the part of him still able to reason, that she would resist his kiss. Instead she'd responded with a passion that made him wonder how he would survive without kissing her again. And again.

He went in search of her mouth once more. She'd been about to speak—he caught the word, the sound, with his tongue. He was unsure whether it had been a sigh of pleasure or a murmured no. It mattered not at all, her mouth was his.

Madi stroked her hands up to his shoulders. Again she experienced an overwhelming sensation of belonging, of connection—to this man, this place, and time.

She'd promised herself she would never feel this.

Her heart began to rap against the wall of her chest. Was this how it had been with her mother? Was this how it began?

Yes.

Panic curled through her. Choices. They were hers to make, good or bad, disastrous or not. It wasn't too late.

She fought back the panic, the sense of inevitability and belonging. And she fought it from showing. She couldn't let him see how big a chink he'd put in her armor. He was a man who couldn't be trusted with her weaknesses.

As she started to push him away, he ended the kiss.

Madi drew a deep, steadying breath. A week ago she had considered this man manageable. That word seemed ludicrous now. Ridiculously naive. Dangerous was a better description, much better. She knew what she had to do.

She managed a teasing smile. "It's a good thing I flunked your test. Things could have gotten complicated."

Lance searched her face for a glimmer of the woman he'd held in his arms a moment ago. He wondered if he'd imagined her, but knew he had not. And it grated, unreasonably, that she had so much control when he had none.

He caught her wrist and ever so softly trailed his thumb over the sensitive flesh. Her pulse throbbed beneath his caress, and he smiled with satisfaction. She wasn't as indifferent as she would like him to believe. "You're right, Madi. It could have gotten terribly . . . complicated. But sex"—he brought her wrist to his mouth, then met her eyes once again—"and sexual attraction didn't make my list of importants."

He pressed his lips against her raging pulse, then dropped her hand. "It's too bad. I would have liked to make love with you very much. Come, let's go back."

Madi searched for a snappy response, something that would put him in his place. She found nothing but a whimper. So she followed him, weak-kneed and breathless, furious at her own silence.

Grateful for the time and distance from Lance, Madi hung back a little on the ride to the condos. The night air, decidedly chilly now, cleared her head. And as her head cleared, her determination grew. Lance Alexander would not have the last word, not this time.

They reached the boardwalk, dismounted the bikes, then crossed the wood planks in silence. Lance insisted on walking her to her door, and she acquiesced easily. Once there, she turned to him with her most winning smile.

"You know, Lance, I've been thinking. It seems to me you might be able to use the help of a professional in your search for Mrs. Right."

"A professional?" he repeated, narrowing his eyes.

"Mmm." She flipped her hair over her shoulder. "I think I know what you're looking for—two kids, one dog, a station wagon, and white picket fence. The *Leave It to Beaver* lifestyle." She opened her door and ducked inside. "I'm not a professional matchmaker in the strictest sense of the word, but I am wonderful at putting the right person with the right job. I'll keep my eyes open for you." She shut the screen door and turned off the light. "Good night."

As she walked away Madi heard his muttered oath and laughed to herself. She loved having the last word.

Stop thinking about him, Madi! Just stop.

Madi scowled and slammed the phone back into its cradle. She'd been telling herself the same thing for the last two weeks, and the only thing it had done for her was give her a headache.

She rubbed her temples. Oh, she'd stayed away from Lance. It hadn't been difficult, even though they lived next door to each other. The few times their paths could have crossed on the beach or balcony-to-balcony, she'd made sure they hadn't. She hadn't seen him since the night they'd gone on turtle patrol.

The night he'd turned her upside down with a kiss.

The ache she'd come to expect when she thought of Lance, poignant and gnawing and so sweet it left her palms damp and her mouth dry, curled through her. Who was she trying to kid? It hadn't been difficult dodging him, but staying away had been sheer hell. A thousand times she'd told herself to give in, but a thousand and one times she'd told herself not to.

Madi looked down at the notes littering her desk. It wasn't as if she hadn't had enough to occupy her time. In the last weeks she'd mapped out a schedule of events for the Sea Turtle Society, then had begun matching volunteers with duties. She'd also contacted dozens of businesses about donations—with dizzying success.

Now it was time to present the board with her plans. But first she had to see Lance.

Lance. Her stomach landed with a thud somewhere in the vicinity of her toes. Annoyed with herself, she straightened. Why was she worried? She would discuss her plans with him, treating him like nothing more than a colleague.

She would smile and chat and pretend her world

hadn't been blown apart by the brush of his mouth against hers.

Sure, no problem.

Ignoring the way her fingers shook, Madi gathered together her notes. She had half-a-dozen calls to make, one of them near his office in Cocoa Beach. She would just drop in, hope he was there, and get it over with.

The drive up A1A to Cocoa Beach took only thirty minutes and was pleasant enough. Unfortunately, even with her windows rolled down and radio volume cranked up, she couldn't quell the butterflies in her stomach.

She turned into Florida Coast Construction's parking lot and pulled her rental car to a stop. As she stared at the building, her fingers tightened on the wheel. What if Lance touched her and she didn't have the strength to do anything but melt?

It wouldn't happen. She was an adult woman in control of her emotions and her intellect, not some starry-eyed adolescent who still believed in happy-ever-afters and knights in shining armor.

Resolutely pushing away remembrances of wishes made on full moons and aches felt with infants in her arms, she collected her briefcase and stepped from the car.

Florida Coast Construction's offices were amazingly uncorporate in appearance. The outside was traditional Florida stucco, low slung with lots of windows and balconies. The interior—at least the large, light lobby she was standing in—was even more unusual. White wicker furniture and an overabundance of plants and floral-patterned pillows lent the interior a lush, tropical feel. The tile floor was the color of sand and scattered with brightly woven area rugs.

Madi crossed to the receptionist's desk. "Hi." She sent the woman a hundred-watt smile. "I'm looking for Mr. Alexander's office."

The woman returned her smile. "Down the hall and to the right."

Lance's secretary wasn't so easily charmed. "He's in conference."

Madi's smile didn't waver. "Could you please tell him that Madison Muldoon is here, and that it's important I speak with him."

"I'm sorry. You don't have an appointment and he asked not to be disturbed."

Madi turned the wattage up a little. "No problem, I understand, orders from the boss and all that." She turned to leave, then stopped, inspecting several photos on the woman's desk. "Are these your cats? They're adorable! I travel so much I can't keep them, but growing up . . ."

Five minutes and much discussion about feline peculiarities later, Madi was being ushered into Lance's office.

"It figures you'd get by Bernice," he said, tossing his pencil down. "Nobody else does."

Madi smiled and sank into the chair opposite his desk, noting the fatigue lines around his eyes and mouth. Too many late nights, she thought, ignoring a tickle of concern. Serves him right. "It turned out we had something in common, but I promised her I wouldn't keep you."

"Thanks." Lance leaned back in his chair, the leather creaking as he did. "What can I do for you?"

If she'd worried he'd try to remind her of their

shared intimacy on the beach, or attempt to stir up anything between them, she'd wasted her energy. He wasn't just distant with her, he was brusque. She told herself she was relieved. "I have my preliminary schedule of fund-raising events planned and I intend to call a board meeting for early next week. I'd promised you a first look, so . . ." She handed him the list.

He read it, rubbing the bridge of his nose as he did. A minute later, he tossed her schedule back. "This won't work. Not here. Go back to the drawing board."

She stared at him, heat climbing her cheeks. "Pardon me?"

"Your kickoff event." He tapped the paper with his index finger. "This black tie gala, it won't work. And much of your year revolves around its success."

Anger replaced surprise. Madi's mouth thinned as she stood and faced him. "I should have known you'd pull something like this. 'Work together for the good of the Society,'" she mimicked. "What a crock. You've been waiting for an opportunity to stir up trouble."

Lance made an annoyed sound and stood up. "I can see you take criticism like a trouper."

"Can it, Alexander." She collected her notes. "This isn't criticism, this is a reflection of your distrust of fund-raisers. Flat out."

"It's my responsibility to make sure you don't sink the Sea Turtle—"

"I've worked for dozens of charities," she interrupted. "The gala is *always* a success. If you had questioned something else on this list, maybe,

maybe, I would have reconsidered, but not the gala." She stuffed the notes back into her briefcase. "Stick to brick, Alexander, and let me do my job!"

"Madi . . ."

He was around the desk in a flash. He caught her arm a moment before she reached the door. Their eyes met; her skin burned under his hand. She inched her chin up. "Was there something else?"

It was the wrong question. She realized it the second the words landed between them. His eyes lowered to her mouth, and she suddenly couldn't breathe. She wanted him to kiss her. Badly.

He wanted the same. Just as badly. She saw it as he lifted his smoldering gaze back to hers, heard it in the way his breathing quickened.

The moment stretched into two, into a dozen. The air crackled between them, tension becoming a tangible thing. Just as Madi thought she would explode if he didn't kiss her, he dropped his hand. "No, there's nothing else."

Disappointment and hurt—childish, irrational hurt—barreled into her. She fought letting it show. Without looking back, she strode from the office.

Lance watched her go, muttering an oath under his breath. Madison Muldoon was driving him crazy.

A moment ago he'd wanted her mouth against his with a desperation that had made him forget everything but the way she had felt in his arms, warm and pliant and exciting. And the way he'd felt when he'd held her—twenty again and ready to conquer the world.

He hadn't been able to put her out of his head.

Not for an hour, not for a minute. It was ridiculous. She wasn't the woman for him. Her beliefs ran counter to his; she planned never to marry. He couldn't afford the distraction right now.

But he *was* distracted, damn distracted. He raked a hand through his hair. He never should have given in to the crazy temptation to kiss her in the first place. It was easy to discount sexual attraction when coldly making lists, but when faced with remembrances of a mouth that tasted like heaven and a feeling that would surely bound him for hell, it was impossible.

What was he going to do?

He pulled a hand through his hair once more. The first thing he'd have to do was find her and repair the damage he'd done. He hadn't meant to be so short with her. He was tired and frustrated and on edge . . . and he hadn't had a decent night's sleep since their evening on the beach.

Dammit. He rubbed his temple. He didn't have time for this. Several of FCC's big projects, including the Dickerson complex, had run into major snags. The concrete workers' strike put one of his jobs at a standstill, and his company had been underbid twice this month.

Lance scowled. And the only thing he could think of was the look in Madi's eyes the moment before she'd turned and walked away. He swore again, then shouted for Bernice to bring him a cup of coffee and two more aspirin.

It was nearly ten P.M. by the time Lance pulled into his driveway. Grabbing his sack of take-out food, he started inside, only to hear Madi's screen door slam shut. Having a pretty good idea of where she was headed, he started toward the beach.

He'd been correct. "Hi, Hollywood."

She turned at the sound of his voice. She wore a pair of faded blue jeans and a bright red T-shirt. Sitting on the beach, her hair pulled back into an untidy ponytail and toes buried in the sand, she looked about eighteen and irresistible.

And less than pleased to see him. He sat beside her anyway.

Madi looked pointedly at the bag of food. "That stuff will kill you."

"So will starvation. And starvation would be a lot faster and a lot more uncomfortable. Besides"— he unwrapped the burger—"I would think after this afternoon you'd be looking for ways for me to die."

"True," she murmured. "But death by Jolly Burgers just doesn't have the right ring. I've been toying with 'bludgeoned with "to do" lists' and 'strangled with a black tie.'"

"Either has a nice touch."

"I thought so."

They fell silent and for long moments gazed out at the ocean. Then Lance turned back to her. "My given name is Lancelot Heathcliff Alexander."

She stared at him for a full ten seconds before she smiled. "You're joking."

"Would I joke about a name like that?" He crumpled the burger's wrapper and dropped it into the bag. "My mother named me after her two favorite romantic heros. I was ten before I realized I wasn't really a knight."

He saw the moment she forgave him. Her mouth softened, her eyes crinkled, just a bit, at the corners. In that moment, he wanted to kiss her. Kiss her hard . . . and soft. And for a very long time.

"How can I stay annoyed with you now?" She laughed and helped herself to a french fry. "You're not playing fair, Lancelot."

"A man has to use whatever he's given—"

"Even if it's only a corny name."

He laughed with her, relaxation easing through him for the first time that day, maybe in several. "You caught me at a bad time this afternoon."

"Oh?" She snitched another fry.

"Business has been tough lately—strikes, younger, hungrier competitors with less overhead, dumb mistakes. I guess what I'm trying to say is, my delivery today could have used a little work."

"Is that it?"

"No." He closed his eyes and drew a deep breath, not sure why he was telling her all this. He owed her an apology, an explanation, but nothing more. For some reason he wanted to share something of himself with her.

The truth of that scared him senseless.

He began to talk. "My mother worked in a steno pool during the day and, to make ends meet, she cleaned offices at night. Friday nights she cleaned a business called Dickerson Industries. Their offices took her longer than any of her other jobs and she never got home until after I was already in bed. It always seemed wrong that she, we, didn't get to enjoy Friday nights like other people. It seemed wrong that she had to work that night, when the rest of the world was relaxing after a long week."

He met her eyes. "I've been hired to create Dickerson's new office building. Today I almost lost the job. That it was somebody else's screwup doesn't matter. I can lose other contracts, but not that one."

Madi drew her knees to her chest and rested her chin on them. "I hate it when I start to think you're not a total jerk."

"Yeah, me too." He paused for a moment, then said, "I apologize for this afternoon. Not for what I said, but for how I said it."

"Apology accepted." She tipped her face toward his. "What now? In case you haven't noticed, we're in a deadlock."

"Spend the weekend with me."

Her eyebrows shot up. "I thought I was out of the running."

He laughed. "Spend the weekend with me and I'll *show* you why your gala won't work."

"And if I'm not convinced?"

"I'll butt out, totally."

This time she laughed. "I'm not sure I buy that either, but it's worth a shot." She stood and brushed the sand off the seat of her pants. "Don't call too early, I like to sleep-in Saturday mornings."

Five

Lance called early anyway.

Madi pushed the hair out of her eyes and scowled at him. "Do you have any idea what time it is? Seven-fifteen. Not a during-the-work-week seven-fifteen, but a Saturday morning, I-could-have-slept-till-noon seven-fifteen."

"You don't say." He grinned and slipped his hands into the pockets of his khaki shorts. Skimming his gaze over her, he took in her tangled hair and outrageous sleep shirt. "'Cowboys Do It in the Saddle,' Madi?"

She looked down at the oversized T-shirt, then folded her arms across her chest, scowling again. "A gift from a friend who lives in Texas. She thought I'd think it was funny."

Lance could tell from her eyes that she *had* thought it funny. Surprisingly, he did too. He stepped around her and inside. "Should I take your appearance to mean you're not quite ready?"

77

Madi whirled, glaring at him. No one should be able to look so good or be so awake so early in the morning. "Are you always this obnoxious?"

"Always."

He flashed her a wicked smile and her heartbeat doubled. At this rate she'd be awake in no time at all. Blasted man.

She tipped her chin up. "Well, Lancelot Heath-cliff Alexander, you'll just have to wait while I get ready." She started toward her bedroom, calling over her shoulder as she did, "And as long as you're here, you might as well make yourself use-ful. I take my coffee strong and black."

Thirty minutes later Madi stepped into the kitchen, showered, dressed, and ready for what-ever Lance threw her way. Well, almost anything, she thought, catching her breath when she saw him. He was leaning against her counter reading the paper, a cup of coffee at his side, his posture totally relaxed and totally masculine. Swearing at her fluttering pulse, she told herself she'd better get a grip, or this would be a long—and hot—weekend.

"Ready," she said.

He looked up, studying her from her white sneakers, up the brightly patterned capri pants to the cutaway shirt that was cinched at the waist and exposed a small sliver of tanned flesh, until he met her eyes.

"You certainly are," he said softly.

Madi wasn't sure if it was the way his eyes heated, the brandy-smooth tone of his voice, or the seductive curving of his lips that she felt down to the tips of her toes. But whatever it was—and Lord help her if it was all three—she was in deep, deep trouble.

"Coffee." He held out a cup.

She grabbed it as if it were a lifeline. She sipped, then sighed. It was strong enough and black enough to be the devil's own brew. "I take back some of the nasty things I thought about you. You make a mean cup of java, Lancelot."

"Thanks." He indicated a framed five-by-seven of a gorgeous woman wearing a satin evening gown. "This must be your mother."

"That's her. A knockout, isn't she?"

"Mmm." She was, Lance thought. But Madi was more so. There was something untouchable, even cold, about her mother's beauty. Not Madi's. Madi was earthy and warm and way too touchable. And for that very reason he would keep his distance.

He shifted his gaze to another photograph. "Who's this?"

"My sister Tina. That guy with her is the person she married."

"You don't like him?"

"Jim's okay."

He moved to the next photograph.

"Cute baby. Theirs?"

"Yes." Madi smiled. "Morgan Raye. She's three months old now." Madi picked up the photograph, lightly touching the glass with her index finger. "I never knew babies could be so . . ."

She realized what she was doing and set the photo down. She'd thought she was over this stupid "biological clock" thing.

Pretending nonchalance, she started collecting items she would need for the day. "I thought we might go to the beach, so I packed a tote. What do you think about . . ."

Lance drew his eyebrows together as he watched her whirl about the kitchen. This wasn't the kind of woman who chattered, yet here she was, chattering about nothing at all. She had also seemed a forthright person, a person who didn't evade or pull punches. Until a moment ago. "What were you about to say, Madi?"

She looked up at him, feigning confusion. "About what?"

"Babies."

"Oh." She stuffed a bottle of tanning lotion into her tote, cursing him for seeing too much . . . and seeing around her smoke screen. She would have to try harder, she decided, and threw him a brilliant smile. "That I didn't know they could be so . . . neat."

Lance frowned. In a pig's eye. She'd been about to say something else, something much more revealing. It wasn't his business; he should leave it alone. He'd always had a problem leaving stones unturned, though. "Apparently your sister doesn't share your aversion to commitment?"

Madi's fingers froze on the beach towel she'd been folding, but only for a second. Taking a deep breath, she forced herself to look up at him and smile. "I don't know what you mean, Lance. I believe wholeheartedly in commitment. In my business you have to."

That wasn't what he'd meant; she knew that. He let it drop anyway—for now. "Have you done any sailing?"

Madi worked to hide her relief at the change of subject. "A little. Why?"

"A friend of mine owns a racing yacht. How would you like to help crew in a regatta?"

"Sounds like a challenge. I warn you, though, I'm no expert."

"That's okay. He's shorthanded today and this isn't an important race." Lance lifted his coffee cup but didn't drink. Instead he met her eyes over the rim of the cup. "Most of the women wear bathing suits, but Captain Jack will have my head if you show up wearing that green thing."

Madi arched an eyebrow, amused. "Captain Jack?"

Lance laughed. "He's the owner of the boat and takes this racing stuff seriously. A major distraction like—"

"My green thing?"

"Exactly. It wouldn't be a big idea."

She pulled a relatively conservative one-piece out of her tote bag. Dangling it from one finger she held it up for him. "This okay?"

He eyed the minuscule bit of bronze-colored spandex, almost choking on his sip of coffee. Coughing, he glanced from her to the suit and back. "That fits?"

"Like a glove."

Lance swallowed. That's what he was afraid of. "Maybe we should try something else. You know, crewing can test even the thickest skin. Even though this is a minor race, to these people winning is everything. It can get pretty intense out there, and the softhearted or sensitive—"

"Of which I'm neither."

Although he wanted to, Lance really couldn't argue with that. He sighed. Jack *would* have his head—if the boom didn't get it first.

It took no time at all for Madi to see what Lance had meant about the softhearted and sensitive. She was badgered, ridiculed, and cursed at for not reacting quickly enough to the cacophony of shouted commands. But she wasn't singled out. There were a couple of other rookies on board who received the same treatment. Madi took it in stride, yelling right back if she felt the abuse wasn't warranted.

Besides, she thought wryly, a few shouted insults were nothing compared to the reaction she had working alongside Lance. He didn't don a bathing suit, instead just whipping off his shirt and working barechested. And his chest was glorious. Well-muscled with only the smallest scattering of hair, his was the kind of chest a woman could spend hours exploring with the flat of her hands or the very tips of her fingers.

To make matters worse, each time he reeled in a line, his muscles bunched then eased, and his skin, already slick with sweat and salt water, became slicker still.

And the more distracted she became, the more she was yelled at.

Of course, she wasn't the one whose head barely missed a meeting with the boom. Lance ducked just in time, but for the remainder of the race he took serious ribbing from the rest of the crew, particularly Captain Jack.

Wind Spirit took third and afterward the entire crew went out for beer and sandwiches. The good-natured insults and ribbing continued, and Madi had a great time watching Lance squirm. She discovered he blushed—just a little—when he was embarrassed.

Later that night, she couldn't help teasing him about it.

She was curled up on the end of her couch, a glass of wine balanced on her knee. "You seem like a pretty experienced sailor, Lance."

"I've done quite a bit, although I didn't get into it until a couple of years ago."

"Mmm . . ." She sipped her wine, studying him from beneath half-lowered lids. He hadn't made a pass at her, not once all day. She'd expected something, a little gesture, an accidental brush of his hand against her thigh . . . an honest to goodness lunge. Instead he'd been a perfect gentleman.

She frowned. Had she expected it or wanted it? The answer to that didn't bear contemplation. "I would have thought watching out for the boom would have been one of the first things you'd learn about sailing." He shot her an irritated glance, and she laughed. "You're doing it again."

"What?"

"Blushing."

His expression went from irritated to outraged male. "Not a chance."

"I noticed it this afternoon. It's quite delightful. Really."

"Is that so?" Lance set his wineglass with deliberate care on the coffee table. "I imagine," he murmured, standing and starting toward her, "that you blush quite nicely yourself." He placed one hand on either side of her head, trapping her between him and the couch. "I imagine, too, that I could make you blush in any number of"—he leaned toward her—"delicious places untouched by the sun."

Mouth dry, pulse fast, she stared up at him. Lord help her, but he could. Already, she felt as if her skin were on fire and he hadn't even touched her.

He moved even closer. "Shall I prove it?"

Madi tipped her head back; she parted her lips. The phone jangled.

Saved by a cliché. Madi assured herself it was relief, not disappointment, she felt as she ducked past Lance's arms and caught the phone on the fourth ring.

"Mom!"

Lance drew a deep breath and dragged his hands through his hair. So much for knowing what was best for him, he thought. So much for control. First the boom, now an unrelieved ache that had him feeling like a fourteen-year-old with a dog-eared girlie magazine. Damn.

"What do you mean you're getting married again? I didn't know you were getting divorced."

At Madi's tone, Lance turned toward her. She stood ramrod straight, her fingers curled so tightly around the phone cord, her knuckles were white. Wild color flamed in her cheeks.

"Mother, have you thought about . . . I know you're a grown woman, but really, eight . . . okay, seven, but who can keep count?"

There was a long pause, then Madi sighed.

"All right then, I wish you the best of luck. Call me when you get back. Yes, I still love you. You too. Bye." She softly replaced the receiver.

Lance's heart went out to her. She looked frustrated and stricken and . . . lost. He handed her a fresh glass of wine. "Maybe this time it'll work out."

She shook her head. "It never does. I gave up hoping on number four or five." She drained the glass, then set it back down and turned away from him. "I have this memory of her, this picture in my head. She's laughing as she cuts her wedding cake. Outfitted in lace and pearls, she's as beautiful as any princess from any fairy tale. Then I have another mental picture of her, crumpled in a heap on her bed . . . sobbing, her makeup streaked, her expression hopeless."

Madi rubbed her upper arms. "It's like her life has gotten stuck between those two frames and she keeps bouncing back and forth, back and forth."

"She's right, you know. She's a grown woman."

"I know." Madi gazed out the window. "But it hurts, seeing someone you care about make the same mistake over and over again. She needs love and tenderness, she needs approval. But she keeps marrying men who can't give her either. Between marriages she always seemed so much more . . . hopeful. Younger. Less jaded." Madi laughed self-consciously. "Sorry, this must all be boring to you."

It wasn't because he cared about Madi, cared about what made her hurt. He was fascinated

because by understanding her family, he understood her more.

The more he understood, the more he knew she
wasn't the woman for him. And the more he
wished she was.

He closed the distance between them and
cupped her face in his hands. "I better go."

"Yes."

"Will you be able to sleep?"

"I don't know."

The words, the question trembled on the tip of
his tongue: *Would you like me to stay?* Even
though he suspected she might say yes, he knew
staying would be wrong—for them both.

"Try," he whispered, lowering his mouth to hers.
"I have a big day planned for us tomorrow."

He brushed his lips against hers, lightly and
with a tenderness that unnerved him, then let her
go. "Good night, Hollywood."

Without another glance, he let himself out.

They spent the next day exploring the stretch of
beach known as the Space Coast, so-called because of its nearness to Cape Canaveral and the
Kennedy Space Center, jumping into a volleyball
game at one point, betting on a surf contest at
another. While exploring, they visited many shops,
including a haute-couture boutique Lance had
insisted on going into. They ate lunch at a down-
home restaurant that served delectable seafood.

Never once during the weekend did Lance mention the Sea Turtle Society or the reason they were
spending this time together.

He hadn't had to. Early Sunday evening Madi hiked her tote bag a little higher on her shoulder and watched Lance as he bought them ice cream cones from a boardwalk vendor. She understood now. Where California ran the gamut from diamonds to rhinestones to jams, the Florida Coast was strictly casual. Even in the finest restaurants, the majority of the diners dressed casually, and if there was any dress code, it required only sunglasses and tanning oil.

Madi shook her head. He'd been right. Her black tie gala wouldn't attract the number of patrons required to get her year off to the walloping start she needed.

Lance turned to her then and smiled, holding up a triple-dip ice cream cone. She smiled back, the now familiar fluttering in her stomach. Lance had been a fun companion. That this man could have so much energy and such a nose for fun was totally unexpected.

And the night before, when he'd tenderly brushed his lips against hers, it had taken all her strength of will not to cling to him and beg him to stay the night. If she had, she knew she wouldn't have regretted it.

The truth of that stole her breath. Her attraction to him she could handle. She'd lived long enough and seen enough to know the stupidity of letting hormones rule the head. Yet in the last couple of days, she'd found that she liked Lance. A lot. That was dangerous. That, she feared, she couldn't control.

Recriminations and fears dissipated as he returned with their mammoth ice creams. She laughed as he handed her one of them. "It's a good thing I didn't wear 'that green thing,'" she said. "This could be embarrassing."

Lance slid his gaze down her body, encased in the bronze-colored suit. Cut high on the hip and low in the back, the suit revealed every one of Madi's sins. She had none.

"Would you like to walk along the beach?" he asked.

She nodded and they headed toward the water. For once, the breeze off the ocean was tame, almost lazy, and the waves followed suit, lapping at the shore with no more energy than she and Lance lapped their cones.

After several minutes of silence, Lance murmured, "I haven't spent a weekend like this since I was a boy." He furrowed his brow in thought. "I must have been about thirteen the last time. My mother took a weekend off and we played. We didn't have much money to spend so we did things like this—ate ice cream cones and took long walks together on the beach."

"You loved her a lot, didn't you."

He met her eyes. "More than anything."

Silence fell between them once more. Finally, after they'd walked for some time, Madi asked, "What did you do on weekends if not have fun? You were a teenager. Surely beach parties and surfing and girls—"

"I worked," he said shortly. "I had my first full-time summer job the year I turned fourteen. I had to lie about my age on the application, but we needed the money . . . and I wanted to go to college someday."

Madi thought of her own childhood, with all its excesses. "Tina and I had everything, beautiful dresses, dolls, real china tea-sets. I had a pony. It must have cost my parents a fortune to keep it in Hollywood and I hardly ever rode her." She tossed what was left of her ice cream in a trash can they passed. "We lived like princesses."

"Tough life."

"It was." She laughed self-consciously. "That sounds so shallow, like the poor little rich girl. But there's horrible pressure in that type of lifestyle. Everyone, even children, are expected to look and act just so. You're judged by the number of things you have, by the people you know. I feel incredibly fortunate that I found fund-raising. So many people I knew back then are just floundering—drugs, alcohol, bad relationships." She shook her head. "Tina and I were lucky."

Lance squinted out at the ocean, then walked toward its foaming edge. Madi followed, and they stopped where the water could rush over their toes.

"I never floundered," he said, not looking at her. "I've known what I wanted for as long as I can remember."

Madi turned to him. She wasn't surprised by his admission. This was a man who methodically pursued his dreams, a man who understood work but not whimsy, perseverance but not passion.

No, she wasn't surprised, but she was moved— deep down, in a place she had scrupulously guarded for as long as she could remember.

She lifted a hand, wanting to touch him, but she held back, afraid of what one touch would lead her to. "What did you want, Lance?" she asked, her voice almost breathless.

He met her gaze. His eyes had darkened with the approaching twilight, and Madi told herself that the romantic, the poet, she saw reflected in their depths was an illusion.

"I wanted not to be a bastard," he said softly. "I wanted to be the knight I was named for."

Her breath caught. She'd thought she'd liked him before, had thought then that she was in danger. But danger spoke of the possibility for trouble, of threat. Past danger now, she was smack dab in the middle of something she didn't know how to free herself from.

She feared she couldn't go back. Not ever.

She curled her fingers into her palms, battling the need to touch him, battling against the yearning, the ache. Now, at this moment, she wanted to pull him inside of her, hard and deep, so that she and this man would be one. She didn't care about where they were or who might see. She didn't give a damn about the consequences.

The truth of that terrified her. But terror was a whimper compared to the other feelings barreling through her.

"The knight in shining armor who charged in and saved the day," she said, just as softly. "A nice thing to want to be."

"Yes," he murmured, his voice thick. He cupped her face, trailing his thumbs ever so lightly across her lips. "My mother believed in knights in shining armor. She died waiting for hers."

Madi tipped her face into his caress. "My mother believed too . . . only she saw every rich man as ners. She realized too late that their shining armor was an illusion, her dream a prison."

Lance tangled his fingers in her hair. "You found fund-raising, Madi. But what did you want?"

She shut her eyes, sensation and need racing through and filling her. She thought briefly of choices and of self-preservation, then opened her eyes to meet his, steadily and without subterfuge. "All I ever wanted was love and attention."

He loosened his fingers and let his hands drop to her shoulders, then skimmed them down her arms until he caught her hands. "Come."

Lacing his fingers with hers, he led her into the ocean. The water was cold, but did nothing to cool her. If anything it heightened her senses. She became aware of the smell of salt in air, of the poignancy of the fading color on the horizon . . . of each brush of Lance's skin against hers.

And she became aware of her body in a way she never had before. Of the perfection of it, of the miracle of creation, of the completeness of man and woman together. In that moment she existed not of herself, but only in her need for him.

They stopped before the water reached her waist, yet the waves rolling to the shore soaked them both. Without speaking, they faced each other.

The beach had cleared. It was too late for the sun worshippers, too early for the after-dinner walkers. They were, for all intents and purposes, alone.

With the tip of his index finger, Lance caught a droplet of water that trembled on the side of her breast. He brought his finger to his mouth.

Madi's muscles liquified, but still she didn't

touch him, didn't sag against him. He lifted his hands so that only his palms touched the hardened tips of her breasts.

"You don't fit into my plans."

She bit back a sound of pleasure. "Nor you in mine."

He moved his hands in slow circles, just brushing her tautened nipples. She swayed toward him until his hands fully settled over her breasts. He held them there for a moment, then slid his hands up, his fingers curling around her neck and tangling in her hair. "Then what are we doing?"

"I don't know." She touched him then with a greediness she'd never experienced before. It was as if her body knew that sensation was for now and that soon, so soon, all she would be able to do was think. And regret.

She arched her back, pressing herself against him. He was hard with arousal, just as she was wet with it. Her nipples pressed against his chest; his fingers tightened in her hair. "But I don't want to know," she said. "Not yet. Kiss me, Lancelot Heathcliff Alexander. Kiss me now."

He did as she demanded.

Lance lowered his mouth to hers, growling with pleasure, with satisfaction, as he did so. Her mouth was open and ready. Her tongue met his eagerly, even desperately.

Yet as she clung to him—and he to her—he sensed the same vulnerability, the same tentativeness in her kiss as the last time. It lurked under the heat, just beyond the passion, and it touched him in a way the other could not. He tightened his fingers in her hair and wondered if he would ever be able to let her go.

Madi curled a leg around his, anchoring him to her. He tasted of salt water and ice cream. His skin, like hers, was hot despite the water. This felt right, so right.

The sense of belonging was new, as was the desire. It frightened her in a way loneliness did not, in a way thoughts of the future had never been able to. To feel so much, to want so much, was to have too much to lose. She tightened her fingers in his hair and deepened the kiss.

A wave, larger than the last, surged against them. It lifted them, but since they were pressed together as one, it didn't take them. Madi gasped for air as Lance dragged his mouth from hers to her cheek, her throat.

And then he was only holding her, his breathing harsh against her ear, his heart thundering against her chest. She knew it cost him much to stop, because she, too, felt like she was about to die.

She loosened her fingers, then combed them through his wet hair. "Your hair is as silver as it is blond," she whispered, her voice husky with passion.

"It's always been that way." He released a long, shuddering breath. "My mother used to say it was silver to go with my armor."

Madi dropped her hands to his shoulders, smoothing the water away. "She never regretted—"

"No. I'm certain of that."

"How wonderful for you." She tipped her head

back to look at him. "I think my mother regretted everything. She still does."

"And what of you, Madi? What do you regret?"

She lowered her eyes. That they weren't making love, that they were an impossible combination in an impossible situation. She lifted her gaze to his once more. "I think you know."

"Yes." He brushed his thumb slowly across her lips. "Yes, I know." He dropped his hands; he stepped away. "We should go."

"Yes." Now was the time for rational thought, she knew, for the beginnings of regret. Hurt and denial swelled inside her. She fought them back.

"Would you like to grab a bite to eat on the way home?" he asked.

She felt suddenly bereft and cold. Wrapping her arms around herself, she shook her head. "No. The ice cream filled me up."

He held her elbow to steady her as they exited the water. He released her the moment they were free of the waves. They showered and dressed there at the beach. The ride back to the condos passed in awkward silence.

Madi sneaked a peek at Lance from the corners of her eyes and wished she knew what he was thinking. Or maybe she didn't, she decided. Her own regret was difficult enough to deal with. His would be the final blow.

When he walked her to her door it was still early, not quite eight o'clock. She took her keys from her beach bag and looked at him, then asked the question she knew she should not but that she couldn't hold back. She wasn't ready for their weekend, or this night, to end. "Would you like to come in?"

Lance stared at her for a long moment, then slipped his hands into his pockets. "I can't. I have plans."

"Oh." She fumbled with the keys a moment, feeling foolish.

"It's something I set up early last week. . . ." He let his voice trail off. "I had fun this weekend, Madi. And it's been a long time since I've had fun."

"I did too."

He touched her cheek, just once, lightly. "I have to get on with my plans."

She knew then what he meant—he had to get on with his plans for finding a wife, for creating his perfect little family unit. It shouldn't matter to her, it shouldn't hurt.

It cut like a knife anyway.

She shrugged with seeming carelessness. "A prospective Mrs. Alexander? Good luck."

Lance swore silently. Already she was fitting her walls back into place. He wasn't sure why that annoyed him so, but it did. "I'm taking her on a turtle walk."

Madi's fingers froze on the key as anger washed over her. She battled to keep it from showing. "I would have thought even you could be a little more original, Lance."

His jaw tightened at her tone. "Meaning?"

"Turtle walks. I'll be sure to keep off the beach at night."

He caught her arm as she started to duck inside. "Our turtle walk was business-only, Madi."

"So's the one you're about to go on now, Lance."
She slipped inside. "Good night."

For long moments Lance stood on her patio,
staring at her closed door before he headed across
the lawn to his.

Why had he lied to her?

He bit off a curse of frustration as he unlocked
the door of his own condo. He should have a date.
He'd found plenty of suitable women. But he had
compared each one to Madi . . . and each one
had paled with the comparison.

He sighed and flipped on a light. He'd lied
because the last thing he'd wanted to do was leave
her. And because she had him forgetting about
lifelong plans and thinking instead about a wild
romance with a totally unsuitable woman.

He'd lied because he was in deep trouble and he
needed time—and space—to figure a way out of it.

Six

"As you see, I've proposed four major fund-raising events for this year—one for each season." Madi smiled at the boardmembers, making sure she made eye contact with each of them.

With the exception of Lance. Lance's gaze she studiously avoided.

Several days had passed since she'd bid him good-night at her back door. In that time she'd fumed over his arrogance, over the fact that he could leave her company—her arms—and go right to another woman. And she'd fretted, because despite the righteous indignation she told herself she felt, she hadn't been able to put him, or their passionate embrace, out of her mind.

"Both the road race and sailing regatta," she continued, as if her thoughts weren't being pulled in a completely different direction, "are perfect spring events. The advertising people will come up with official tag lines, but I envision something like Race For the Turtles.

"Winter lends itself to golf, again because of the weather. I thought a Southern-style barbeque afterward would be fun, complete with country music and square dancing."

Lance was staring at her. She felt his gaze burning into her, demanding she look at him. She straightened her shoulders almost imperceptibly and met his eyes. She would not be bullied!

He smiled a small, knowing smile and she silently cursed him. He was purposely trying to rattle her. And doing a good job of it. Blasted man!

She cleared her throat and wondered if there was any way she could arrange for the earth to open up and swallow Mr. Lance Alexander.

Even as she did, she continued, not missing a beat. "I planned the fall event around Halloween. Respect for the environment needs to be learned at an early age, so I've scheduled events for the entire family throughout the week of and before Halloween. Patrons will be able to purchase 'package' tickets as well as tickets for individual events only."

She slipped her hands into the pockets of her cotton knit jacket. "For example, I've scheduled a hayride and a haunted house for the kids, adolescent and adult scavenger hunts, and a murder mystery party for adults who fancy themselves detectives.

"I've already contacted one of the local cruise ships, and they're willing to donate the boat for the mystery party in return for the food and liquor business. Of course, there are many land locations that would be suitable as well, most notably your famous 'Island House.'"

The boardmembers smiled and nodded with approval to one another, but Lance's expression revealed nothing. Madi narrowed her eyes, just a little. He was no doubt waiting to see what she'd done—if anything—with her black tie gala.

"And now for our kick-off event, which will take place at the soonest possible date." She met Lance's eyes again, this time in challenge. "I envision a variation on the traditional black tie gala—a black tie beach party. Beach apparel will be the order of the hour; the Society will provide black ties at check-in. We'll set up cabanas on the beach. The music will be calypso, reggae—something with an island beat. Local restaurants will be invited to donate the one dish they're most known for and provide servers. For example, crab cakes from Mariners and chocolate truffles from La Confection."

She drew a deep breath. "I'd like to discuss this in more detail, but I thought we could do so by addressing your questions and comments first."

Thirty minutes later, Madi smiled as the board unanimously approved her proposal. As she began to collect her things, Darnell suggested they all adjourn to a place on the beach for cocktails.

Madi's stomach crashed to her toes and her gaze flew almost unwittingly to Lance. She could hardly refuse, and judging by Lance's expression, he wasn't going to either.

She muttered several curt, colorful words as he started over to her.

"What, no date?" she asked him. She snapped

her briefcase shut with more force than necessary.

He laughed and leaned against the information counter. "I had one but cancelled it. After all, I couldn't miss your proposal."

Madi fought back a sting of irrational jealousy. "Well, I've made it and you've heard it, so why don't you run along to one of your 'Mrs. Alexander' prospects."

"And leave you alone with this gullible group? Not a chance."

Before she could utter the tart reply that sprang to her tongue, Darnell rushed up to her, hands outstretched. "Madison, darling! Wonderful ideas. Pure genius, really."

Madi turned to the flamboyant boardmember. At the same moment another of the boardmembers lassoed Lance. Relief flooded through her. She was off the hook for the moment.

"Darnell, I'm so glad you liked them. I'm pleased myself."

"You should be. And I must say I feel like the hero of the hour for having found you." He lowered his voice and leaned toward her. "And how are you getting along with our director? Isn't he as uptight as I warned?"

Madi peeked at Lance from the corner of her eyes. He looked every inch the uptight, conservative businessman she'd thought him to be when they first met, the same one Darnell had described. But how could that man have touched her heart the way he had? How could he have made her feel things she never had before, not with any man?

How could she say any of that to Darnell Pea-body?

Madi looked back at the older man and smiled with what she hoped was ease and carelessness. "He does have definite ideas about what he wants."

"I picked up some very weird vibes happening between you two. Have you been at each other's throats?"

"You could say that," she murmured, remembering the way she had clung to Lance, remembering the feel of his lips, hot and urgent, against her skin. "But it's nothing I can't handle," she added quickly.

"Of course, my dear. I have complete confidence in you."

Madi caught the speculative gleam in his eyes and slipped her arm through his. "Tell me about this place we're going to."

Darnell ignored her question. "I heard he's joining us. He never does, you know. Odd, don't you think?"

"Not at all," she said blithely. "He probably wants to make sure I don't sneak in some outrageous and costly event when he's not around."

"I'm sure that's it," Darnell murmured, looking as if he didn't believe a word she'd said. He patted her hand. "It's a little place called The Coconut Tree and it's fabulous, just fabulous. I know you're going to love it."

The little place on the beach was just that. Small, with a thatched roof and no walls, it was more a gazebo than anything else. Although their group was a bit crowded around a small table, the fruity drinks were excellent and the scenery was unbeatable.

Madi even began to relax. Lance had chosen a chair several down from hers and had kept up a steady conversation with one of the boardmembers.

Yes, she was relaxed, until everyone began to disappear. First it was Darnell—off in search of love and romance. Then Patricia announced she had to relieve a babysitter, Jed and Nelson both had dates, and Julia had a business engagement.

That left herself . . . and Lance. Madi looked around in stunned disbelief. How had it happened so quickly? A moment ago there had been five adults besides Lance at the table. Now there were none.

She reached for her briefcase. Time for her to exit. "Well, I guess it's getting to be that—"

Lance's hand closed over hers. "Before you go, Madi, I'd like to discuss our working arrangements for the next few weeks."

"Working arrangements?" she repeated, staring helplessly at his hand covering hers.

"You sound surprised. I thought you understood that I wanted to be involved in this project every step of the way."

"But—" She cleared her throat, finding it difficult to focus on anything but the warmth of his hand on hers. "I thought you wanted to be involved in the planning stage. That's done, now it's on to the grind work. And believe me," she said as earnestly as she could, "it's no fun. Lots of paperwork and committee meetings."

He stroked his thumb almost absently across

her knuckles. "I like what you did with the gala. In fact, your whole schedule showed a lot of creativity, a step beyond the usual fund-raising fare."

"Thank you." She forced herself to keep her gaze on him and ignore the sensations his caress stirred inside her. "I told you I was good."

"That you did." He lowered his eyes to her mouth and her breath caught. When he lifted them again, she thought the green of his irises had darkened. She called herself a fool—yet again. "But your work is only partly done," he continued, "and as the Society's director, I feel it's my responsibility to sit in on as many of the committee meetings as my schedule will allow."

She slipped her hand from his. He offered no resistance, and she realized it was the first time she'd tried to break the contact. Heat climbed her cheeks. "Fine," she said. "I'll let you know when they're scheduled with enough time for you to work them into your calendar."

She started to push her chair back.

"And since I'm so busy," he said, "we can get together in the evenings."

"Excuse me?"

"To go over the minutes of the meetings I miss."

She stared at him a moment, then arched her eyebrows in blatant disbelief. His voice and expression were totally innocent, but she would bet money he had more than "minutes" on his mind. "That one's a little corny, even for you, Lance."

"What?"

"That line." She folded her arms across her chest. "Evenings, Lance? Really."

"I assure you, I'm being perfectly sincere." He

grinned wickedly. "We both know the other evening was an . . . aberration. We want different things from life, and the last thing I would do is jeopardize our working relationship."

He called what they shared an aberration? She narrowed her eyes. "Our working relationship, Lance?"

"Of course. The Society comes first."

He sounded Sunday-morning sincere and yet . . .

"Speaking of plans and such," he added, "I've been thinking of taking you up on your offer."

Madi pictured the offer she'd made without words on the beach, the one that had her tossing and turning at night and taking cold showers. "Excuse me?"

"Your offer to help me find a wife," he said blandly. "I could use your input."

"Oh."

"What did you think I meant?"

"Nothing. I didn't know what you meant, that's all." She gritted her teeth. So much for cool and calm and in control.

"So, what do you think?"

"About finding you a wife?"

"Yes."

"I told you before, I think your plan's both distasteful and manipulative."

"Yeah, but I'm not asking you to marry me, just help me find someone else to marry." He flashed her a sexy grin and leaned across the table. "How about her?"

Madi swiveled around. The woman he'd indicated was a flashy redhead in orange hot pants.

Madi looked back at him in disbelief. "Really, Lance, you can't be serious."

He looked tragically disappointed. "No? Well how about her?"

This one was a petite blond with a sparkling smile. She was also, obviously, taken. "Look lower, Lance. She's pregnant."

"Oh." He looked back at Madi. "I don't have a problem with that. Do you think she's married?"

Madi rolled her eyes. "I think so."

He sighed. "Okay, then how about her?"

"Her" was a brunette wearing a Brooks Brothers suit and a Rolex Lady President. Madi shook her head. "No wonder you aren't having any luck. She's too smart, too successful."

He grinned. "That was a shot."

"You got it."

She grabbed her briefcase and slid her chair back, determined that this time he wouldn't stop her. "I suggest simpleminded and plain, Lance. The more of each the better. A woman with other options would never go for your insane plan." She stood. "I'll apprise you of events as they happen. Good night."

As she walked away Madi felt as simpleminded as they came, because, God help her, for a moment there she had considered asking him to let her take his damnable test again.

"I'm going to get some more tea," Lance said, standing. "Do you want anything?"

"No, thanks." Madi watched as he disappeared into her kitchen, then shook her head and helped herself to another piece of the take-out chicken he'd brought with him.

Four weeks had passed since the night of her presentation, and during that time she and Lance had only met twice. Even though she'd ached and pined and made all sorts of silly wishes when they'd been apart, she'd been relieved.

Because when she was with him, as hard as she tried, she couldn't think straight or breathe evenly.

Tonight, though, despite the lack of oxygen to her brain, she had to admit she felt comfortable with him. Dangerously so. Maybe it was the way he sprawled across her living room floor, looking for all the world as if he belonged there, or maybe it was because those last two meetings with him had passed without incident.

Well, that wasn't quite true, she thought, remembering the first meeting. She and Lance had met at the Sea Turtle Society to go over the minutes from three different committee meetings. They'd just about finished when Jenny appeared at their office door, a strange look on her face.

"Uh-oh," she'd murmured.

They'd both looked at the young woman and said in unison, "Uh-oh, what?"

"I think it's time."

Madi felt the blood drain from her face. "The baby?"

Jenny laid a hand on her swollen belly. "It's coming!"

"Are you sure?" Lance asked, standing and crossing to her.

"Yes," she wailed. "It can't come, not now! Rick's

out of town. What am I going to do about a partner?"

It seemed to Madi the "partner" part had been taken care of months ago. "Do you have a number where he can be reached? We'll call him and—"

"He won't make it in time! We did all the classes and had everything planned and now what am I going to do?"

Lance put his arm around the wild-eyed young woman. "I'll do it, Jenny. I've been a Lamaze partner before. Don't worry, everything will be fine."

A Lamaze partner? Madi wondered. Lance? Stunned silent, she followed them outside. She hadn't thought he was capable of surprising her this much. Once again he'd proven her wrong.

Five hours later, Lance came out of the delivery room. He looked exhausted. Madi jumped up and hurried over to him. "Is everything okay?"

"Fine." He rubbed his temples. "It's a boy."

"A boy," she repeated, a catch in her throat. "That's what Rick wanted."

"Did you call him?"

She nodded, swallowing hard. "He's on his way." She clasped her hands in front of her. "I was out of town when Tina . . . went into labor. What was it like, Lance? I mean, was Jenny scared? Did it hurt . . . a whole bunch?"

He smiled and put his arm around her. "Yes and yes," he said gently, "but she's fine. She forgot the pain the moment she saw her baby."

"Oh." Madi looked at him, feeling as though her heart would burst with tenderness. "Where did you learn to do this stuff? You weren't rattled at all, and I thought I was going to faint. I still might."

He toyed with the tips of her hair. "I did this for a friend once. You want to go up to the nursery?"

"I don't think so."

Lance had ignored her and together they'd gone to the nursery to see if they could catch a peek of the infant. Lance had held her close to his side and for a moment, she had felt as if she were the new mother and Lance the devoted husband and father.

Madi shook her head and frowned. Feelings like that would get her into trouble. Big trouble. If anything, the experience should have—

"Penny for your thoughts."

She snapped her head up in surprise. Lance was standing in the doorway, his expression thoughtful. She forced an easy smile. "You'd be losing money on the deal."

"I doubt that." He walked across the room, resuming his place on the floor beside her. "So, are you going to tell me what put the frown on your face?"

"Just mulling over things I still have to take care of before the kick-off."

Lance studied her. A moment ago her expression had held naked yearning. Now it was neutral, her tone nonchalant. Her walls were firmly fixed into place. He fought back frustration. "It looks as if everything's going smoothly." He indicated the various reports spread out on the floor around him. "From what I've seen tonight I'd guess all your preparations will be in place within the next couple of weeks."

"Yes," she said. In two weeks she would be able to totally avoid Lance. But not her birthday. The night of the black tie beach party was also the night of her thirtieth birthday.

"Madi, has something gone wrong with the kick-off?" He sounded concerned.

"No, everything's going great." She smiled reassuringly and wiped her fingers on a paper napkin. "I'm just distracted tonight, that's all."

"I hope it's the company?"

It was. Stretched out on her floor, with his silvery-blond hair tumbled across his forehead and his mouth curved in lazy amusement, he was damn distracting. She'd sooner eat worms than admit it, though. "Sorry."

"I'm wounded."

"I'll bet."

"He trailed a finger lightly over her knuckles. "I hear you've gone out on some of the group turtle patrols."

"And a couple rescue missions as well." She swallowed. "Actually, I've become a bit of a turtle junkie. I've even started marking nests and charting their progress. Ours is doing fine so far."

As soon as the words were out of her mouth she regretted them. They implied an intimacy between them, and intimacy was the last thing she wanted to infer—especially considering their surroundings and the way his innocent touch had the blood careening through her veins.

Lance considered letting the comment pass, then smiled wickedly. "Our nest, Hollywood?"

She tossed her head, annoyed at his knowing grin. "A knight would have let that pass."

"My armor's a bit tarnished tonight." He leaned toward her, his eyes gleaming. "Brings back memories, doesn't it?"

Memories of his lips against hers, urgent and demanding. Memories of her heart pounding out of control, of her senses swimming with his touch, his taste—

She shook her head to clear it. "You're right, I'll never forget seeing my first turtle."

"You've got me there."

"So," she said quickly, before he could say anything else, "how's your wife-hunting coming?"

Lance frowned, both at her question and the way it grated. "What brought that on?"

"Well, we're friends." She shot him her best "buddies" smile. "And I'm . . . interested. That's all."

Friends? Lance thought. Right. She was using this as a way to keep distance between them and her guard firmly in place. He shouldn't push; he had no right. But he hadn't pushed for four weeks now, and it had been four weeks of hell.

"If you're really interested," he murmured, "I do have a couple of candidates I'd like your opinion of."

Madi's hands curled into fists as she denied that his words had any effect on her. She'd maneuvered herself into this corner and didn't know how to maneuver back out without looking like a total idiot. "Sure. Great."

Lance propped himself up on an elbow and said with what he hoped was altarboy earnestness, "Marilyn is one of my top salespeople. She's bright, hardworking—"

Madi stopped him. "Not a good idea. When you date an employee, you're opening yourself up to all sorts of complications."

"Oh." Despite her businesslike tone, her eyes had heated, her cheeks pinkened. He fought the urge to tumble her into his arms. "Well, then there's Stephanie. She's an executive secretary, has been married twice, and—"

Madi snorted. "Forget it, Lance. You want a forever marriage and this woman has already ended two? Old habits are hard to break."

"Both divorces were the guys' faults."

Madi simply looked at him, and he sighed as if he were hugely disappointed. "Okay, how about Toni? She's twenty-four and—"

"Too young," Madi inserted crisply.

"She's mature for her age."

Madi shook her head. "Lance, be realistic, you're almost forty."

He dragged his gaze from her mouth. "True, but you have to admit she has plenty of childbearing years left."

The pain to her midsection was as swift as it was debilitating. Madi jumped up with her plate and glass and carried them to the kitchen. There, she set them in the sink and turned on the cold water.

"Did I say something that upset you?"

He'd followed her. She didn't turn. "I don't think I want anything more to do with this crazy plan of yours." She held the plate under the stream of icy water. "It was funny at first. I mean, I found the whole thing so ridiculous . . . but it makes me uncomfortable. I don't think I should participate in something I don't believe in, even as a joke."

He took a step into the room. "You brought it up."

"I know. That was a mistake. I—"

"What's really going on here?" He closed the remaining distance between them, settling his hands on her shoulders. Her muscles were rock hard, and he gently massaged them. "Talk to me, Madi."

"There's nothing going on and nothing to say." She shut off the water and turned slowly toward him. "I've told you how I feel. If you can't accept that—"

"Now *that's* the joke, Madi. You never let anyone know what you feel." He grabbed her hands. They were icy from the water and he rubbed them between his. "My comment about children rattled you. Why, Hollywood? Do you want kids? Is there some reason you can't have them?"

She yanked her hands from his. "I told you before, I plan to never marry."

"That's not what I asked."

She swung away from him, furious that he was able to read her so easily, furious that she couldn't do a better job of hiding her thoughts. "I want you to leave, Lance."

Give her what she asked for, Lance told himself. Say good-night and don't look back. He shook his head. He couldn't. What she'd said with words had nothing to do with what she'd said without. And all his "shoulds" couldn't compare with what he felt in his gut.

"What are you running from, Madi? Me? Or maybe it's something else, something like commitment?"

"I'm not running," she said evenly, looking over her shoulder at him. "I asked you to leave. We've discussed the beach party, we've eaten and chatted. It's time for you to go."

"So you can pretend you're not affected by me, that you don't want to be in my arms."

She squeezed her eyes shut. "That's as crazy as your ridiculous plan!"

"Is it?" He grabbed her arms and turned her toward him once more. This time when he caught her hands, he laced his fingers with hers. "I don't think so. I think you want me for yourself."

"You really should consider seeking professional help for this problem of—"

"Furthermore, I don't think you want me to leave at all. I think you want me to stay"— he lowered his voice—"and for us to make love."

The blood rushed to her head until she was dizzy with it. Fighting the sensation, the dizziness, Madi lifted her chin and narrowed her eyes. "You're arrogant and manipulative and self-absorbed. I wouldn't want you if you were the last man on earth."

Her words hit him like a heavyweight's best right hook. Knowing it was time to cut and run, time to forget about her walls and the fascinating woman he'd glimpsed behind them, he hauled her against his chest. "Prove it," he muttered.

His mouth crashed down on hers. Furious, Madi pushed against his chest. He didn't release her, but she didn't wonder why. She may have been pushing at him with her hands, but her mouth, her tongue, strained for more.

Then, even her traitorous hands clutched instead of pushed, her body pressed against instead of pulled away. She shuddered. How could this man take her from anger to passion to contentment in a matter of seconds? And how could he make her feel this soft, this secure and maleable?

This totally out of control.

Madi stiffened at the truth of that. She was so close to making the mistake of a lifetime—the mistake she'd seen made over and over again—she could almost touch it. And no one could save her but herself.

It took every ounce of will she had, but she pushed him away. Panting, she met his eyes. "Please leave. Now."

Lance's breathing was as uneven as hers. "Still running I see."

She balled her hands into fists. "And what of you? What does your rational, levelheaded plan protect you from? Real emotion? Heart?" She tipped her chin up. "Or just good old-fashioned pain? You can't hurt if you don't love, right, Lance?"

Her words hit their mark, and he swore. "Earlier you called this a joke. You were right." He grabbed his jacket from the back of a chair. "See you around, Muldoon."

Madi watched him go, her eyes filling with tears. She wrapped her arms around her middle as she heard the front door slam shut. Joke. It *had* been her word. But jokes were supposed to be funny.

She wasn't amused. She might never laugh again.

She'd done the most stupid thing imaginable—she'd fallen in love with him.

Seven

". . . happy birthday, dear Madi, happy birthday to you."

Madi smiled weakly at the delivery boy's attempt at song, then accepted the huge balloon bouquet he held out to her. Softly shutting the door, she turned and leaned back against it.

Thirty. A three and a zero. How could two such harmless numbers be so unsettling when put together and called age? Madi frowned. Yesterday she had been a two and a nine, and she'd been comforted by that fact. Only a day's difference, yet that day had seemed to allow her so much more time. So many more concessions.

She drew her eyebrows together, tapping one of the shiny Mylar balloons with her finger. It bounced and swayed in response, the curved surface distorting her image like a fun-house mirror.

Disconcerted, she turned her face away. The balloons were from her sister, brother-in-law, and niece. Her mother had sent—appropriately—a huge arrangement of exotic flowers, and had signed her current husband's name to the card as well. Her father had forgotten.

That was it. No calls from old school chums or sorority sisters. No lovers bearing gift-wrapped presents and promises of happy-ever-after—not that she believed in that anyway.

But that wasn't all, Madi thought, shifting her gaze to the fresh-cut flowers she'd placed on the coffee table. Lance had sent the arrangement, not for her birthday but to wish her good luck for that night. Nothing else could have made her feel so bittersweet . . . so alone.

The tears that had been testing her control ever since she'd realized the truth about her feelings for Lance, welled in her eyes, then slipped down her cheeks. Blasted man, why did he have to be sweet? And why now?

In the weeks since their last meeting, she'd tried to reason herself out of the truth. When that hadn't worked, she'd tried pretending and denying. Finally she'd given in and admitted she was in love with Lancelot Heathcliff Alexander.

And that was that.

Except she'd yet to figure out what she was going to do about it.

Nothing, she told herself sternly, ignoring the quick stab of pain. She would do nothing about it. Lance had his path, she had hers. She knew what was right for her even if her heart didn't.

Madi wiped at the moisture on her cheeks. For the first time she understood the plight of her mother and the other women she'd known. Love overpowered good sense, it dulled the instinct for self-preservation. She ached. She burned. She wallowed.

Madi smiled weakly at that. She'd never thought she would be lovesick. She realized now that in the past, when Tina or her other friends had complained of the malady, she'd felt somewhat superior, invincible even. Madi Muldoon, Woman of Steel.

She'd been invincible because nothing she'd ever felt for a man had had anything to do with the real world of men and women and broken hearts. Nothing she'd felt had ever really touched her.

Her feelings for Lance touched her in places and ways that scared her right down to the tips of her toes.

Madi pushed away from the door and carried the balloons from the foyer into her living area. She set them on the coffee table, then looked around the room. Rattan furniture, bright floral pillows, and throw rugs, lots of plants and prints. Someone else's things, someone else's taste. Yet she called this home.

Home for now anyway.

Tears threatening again, she walked into her tiny kitchen, to the refrigerator where magnets held the latest photos of Morgan. The pictures showed the infant in all her latest and greatests— waving her tiny fists, gurgling, and . . . smiling up at Tina with love and trust shining in her eyes.

A trembling sensation started in the pit of her stomach and spread until even the tips of her fingers quivered. Her arms and chest ached; a metallic taste filled her mouth. The taste of wanting.

She turned her back to the photos and pressed the heels of her hands over her eyes. Lance had accused her of running. Was she?

She traveled as a way of life—a year here, a year there. There were no birthday salutations from friends because she moved around too often to make the kind of friends that remembered and acknowledged birthdays. That didn't mean she avoided relationships or was running from commitment. It didn't mean that she kept a part of herself closed off or hidden.

Dammit, she'd made her choices years ago. She knew what would make her happy, but more, what would make her miserable.

So, what was she now?

She shook herself. This had to stop. She wasn't the first woman to fall in love, nor the first to have birthday-blues. She didn't have time to mope or feel sorry for herself. She had a party to attend.

Hoping Lance would decide to stay home that night, she went to dress.

Although Madi hadn't known just what to expect from the gala's attendees in the way of dress, for herself she had chosen a simple black maillot and a short black Hawaiian-style wrap skirt. She'd decided against both shoes and jewelry, but had pulled her hair up into a funky, fun style.

She saw as her guests began arriving that the evening's outfits would run the gamut from conservative to wild, from completely concealing to completely revealing.

Unfortunately, Lance had chosen revealing.

Madi drew a deep breath when he appeared, then started across the sand toward her. His small black racing suit covered everything—and nothing. With a bow tie at his throat, he looked like a Chippendales dancer. Only better. Her temperature rose, her pulse points tingled, and she told herself to keep her eyes fixed firmly on his face.

She immediately caught herself lowering her gaze and muttered an oath. She'd like to throttle Lance for this. He couldn't have chosen baggy trunks or jams? He couldn't have tucked himself into a nice, conservative pair of black shorts and T-shirt?

He smiled as he spotted her, and her stomach turned a quick somersault. *How was she going to work alongside him all evening?*

"Hello, Hollywood."

"Lance." It took everything she had to keep the longing she felt for him out of that one, small word. "You didn't need to come early. My volunteers and I have everything under—"

"I wanted to," he interrupted, his voice seeming huskier than usual. He swept his gaze slowly over her. "You look beautiful."

She glanced down at herself, insecurity warring with surprise. She'd never doubted her looks or appeal, yet the urge to beg him for reassurance raced over her.

The fear of revealing herself was stronger. She flashed him a brilliant, breezy smile. "Thanks, so do you. Look great that is. If you'll excuse me, one of my chairpersons is—"

He caught her arm. "Did you get my flowers?"

"Yes." She cleared her throat. "They were lovely."

"I meant it, you know. Good luck."

"Thanks." She started to pull away. He tightened his grip.

"We need to talk, Madi."

His fingers seemed to burn into her flesh. Ignoring the sensation she met his gaze. "Is there some problem with the party arrangements?"

"No." He lowered his voice. "There's some problem with us."

Us. The word had her heart doing flip-flops. That wouldn't do, not tonight. "Later, Lance," she murmured, a telltale tremor in her voice. "We'll talk later." With that she slipped away.

Later came with a speed that left her breathless.

Madi stood at the edge of the ocean, the cleanup underway behind her, the waves tickling at her feet. The evening had passed quickly and uneventfully. Both she and Lance had had guests to take care of, minicrises to attend to. They hadn't spoken again.

But, as if she were metal and he magnet, she'd been aware of him and drawn to him every single minute—just as she was aware of him coming up behind her now. Fighting the pull all evening had drained her. She had no more fight.

He stopped so close to her that if either one moved a fraction toward the other, they would be touching. Neither did.

"A wishing moon," he said softly.

"Yes," she replied, not turning to him.

"Have you wished?"

"No." She gave her head a small shake. "I haven't the energy, not tonight."

"The party was a huge success," he said after a moment. "I take back every one of my doubts."

"Do you? Even with the rest of the year to go?"

"Yes."

"Better watch out, Alexander. You'll be accused of having a heart."

"Not a chance." He studied her troubled profile, wanting to touch her, wanting to reassure with a caress, to soothe with the brush of his flesh against hers. Instead, he said what he'd come to say. "I'm sorry about our last meeting. I shouldn't have pushed. Considering my plans, I had no right."

Madi squeezed her eyes shut. There he went, being sweet again. Being the kind of man who could love and be loved in return. Being the kind of man she knew didn't exist, not for her.

She met his eyes then. In them she read concern and caring. And awareness. The kind of awareness that promised passion—dark and desperate and sizzling out of control. The kind that offered hope and heaven and a few hours of oblivion. The kind she'd never experienced before.

In that moment, a lifetime of walls fell away and what she had to do, right then, for this night, became crystal clear.

"Today was my birthday," she said softly, slowly.

"Happy birthday."

"I turned thirty today."

"I wouldn't have asked."

"Chivalrous of you." She curled her toes into the

wet sand. "But you could have. I'm not ashamed of my age."

He touched her then, lightly on her cheek. He couldn't help himself. She turned her face into the caress. "But you're not happy about it," he said.

"No, I'm terrified." She covered his hand with hers. "Come home with me, Lance. Stay with me tonight. Make love with me."

Surprise hit him first. Arousal next. For long moments he stared at her, then he shook his head. "I don't think so, Madi." He tenderly cupped her other cheek. "You're vulnerable tonight. Needy. Tomorrow you would regret this, us, and although I want you more than I've ever wanted before . . . I don't want you that way."

She tightened her fingers over his, then released his hand and stepped away. It took everything she had just to look at him. If he touched her again, she would crumble. "You probably think I'm experienced with men. I don't look like a chaste, little virgin. I don't act like one either. Add to that the fact that I'm a star's kid and grew up in Hollywood and you practically have the cliché for 'wild thing.'"

She met his gaze evenly. "Two men, Lance. Just two."

"Madi—"

"Neither man was a one-night stand, nor was the act done . . . irresponsibly. I had my wits about me all the time." She drew a deep, careful breath. "I don't share myself easily. Not in that way, not in any way."

He took a step toward her. "You didn't have to tell me those things, Madi. I never thought you were promiscuous or unsafe. I never thought you were anything but a vital, interesting, and exciting woman. Not a cliché, not a type."

"I did have to tell you," she countered. "Because I want to convince you. I need not to be alone tonight, Lance. I need to feel arms around me, to feel the warmth of another human being."

"And what of tomorrow?"

"Tomorrow I'll be fine—the confident, impenetrable Madi Muldoon. Tomorrow you can call me Hollywood again." She touched his mouth with the tips of her fingers. "But tonight I need you to call me lover."

Her touch raced over him like wildfire. "What about us, Madi?"

"We can go back to being temporary neighbors and cautious colleagues. We both have plans, and neither of us fits into the other's."

She caught his hand and brought it to her mouth. She pressed a kiss in his palm, then let him caress her cheek. "But tonight scares me. I don't think I can face what's left of it alone."

He trailed his thumb across her full lower lip. It trembled under his touch. "I'm not a stud service, Madi. Is it me you want or—"

"No one else would do, Lance." The words caught in her throat. This was the hardest thing she'd had to say. She'd revealed much tonight, but she wouldn't—couldn't—reveal all. Not ever. "I've never wanted anyone, anything, as I want you. I'm not talking commitment or promises—but I know neither would you be. Tonight, Lance. One night of passion, of giving in to what we both know we shouldn't but can't seem to deny."

"And if I say no?"

"Then I'll make do . . . alone."

Lance answered without words. He lowered his mouth to hers, brushing his lips against hers, tasting and soothing, warming but still denying. He lifted his head. "We have to finish here."

"Yes."

When she made a move as if to do just that, he stopped her. He tugged at her topknot of hair, and it tumbled to her shoulders. Tangling his fingers in the silky waves, he murmured, "What would you say if I told you I hadn't been able to look at another woman since I met you, that I'd been unable to sleep, to concentrate on work?"

She kissed the corners of his mouth, not fighting her pleasure at his admission. "I would say that I'm glad. That I hoped I'd made you miserable with longing." She pressed closer against him, lowering her voice to a husky drawl. "And I would say that it makes me feel very powerful, very sexy."

He swept his mouth across hers again, then nipped at her lower lip. "Before you," he murmured, "I told myself passion wasn't important. I told myself that sexual attraction didn't matter in the scheme of things and that I could control it. Then I met you and chemistry controlled me. Suddenly I could think of nothing but making love with a woman with hair the color of caramel, a woman who was cocky and confident and completely out of my league."

"Why are you telling me this?" She searched his expression. "You didn't have to say anything but yes."

"Because I want you to know what I feel for you is special, I want you to know how strongly you affect me. And I want you to know that my plan has been at a standstill since the first time we kissed."

It wasn't love, Madi thought, but it would do in a pinch. Feeling giddy as a schoolgirl, she stood on tiptoes and pressed her mouth to his. Laughing, she whispered, "Let's delegate then, and blow this pop stand, Lancelot."

They ended up at her place. Maybe because he was following her lead, but more likely because it was a few steps closer.

The door clicked shut behind them; Lance turned the lock. They faced each other.

Madi swallowed. Audibly.

Lance smiled. "Am I so terrifying?"

"Yes . . . no . . . yes."

He trailed his fingers across her cheek to her hair. "I could grow to like you this way, Hollywood."

Madi held herself perfectly still, absorbing the heat emanating from his fingertips, letting the sensations they caused skitter over her. "What way is that?" she managed to ask finally.

"Soft and warm . . . dependent." She frowned at that. He rubbed his thumb across the wrinkle that formed between her eyebrows. "Is that so bad? Being dependent sometimes? Needing?"

Madi shuddered as his fingers roamed, then she relaxed and leaned against him. Giving into her need to touch him, to explore his male secrets, she ran her hands across his bare chest, over his shoulders, around to his back. His flesh was different from hers, firmer, more resilient, his contours more angular.

He smelled salty—from the ocean air and his own sweat. She tasted him with the tip of her tongue, here, then there, moving slowly, savoring. He tasted as he smelled. The salt tingled, her pulse soared.

"The day we sailed," she whispered, tilting her head back to meet his eyes, "I wanted to do this so badly. I couldn't concentrate, couldn't seem to keep my mind on what I was supposed to be doing. And because of it, I kept getting yelled at."

He sucked in a sharp breath as she stroked her hands lower. "At least you didn't almost get killed."

She splayed her fingers; the muscles beneath them tightened. "The boom?" She knew she sounded totally female and deliciously satisfied. She didn't mind the stereotype.

"Uh-huh." His lips slid across her cheek, over an eyebrow.

"I'd hoped so." As he found her ear and nipped, the breath hissed past her lips and she arched her back.

"The ribbing I took was the worst. Everyone knew." He laughed softly, nipping her again. "Of course there wasn't a guy on the boat who really blamed me . . . or could keep his own attention on the race."

"We took third."

"We should have had first. Easily."

She laughed and caught his hands. "I'll send my apologies to Captain Jack, but now . . ."

She let her words trail off suggestively and led him from the foyer to her bedroom. She hadn't left any lights burning; she didn't pause to switch any on. The scent of flowers, for one moment, was almost overpowering.

Then they were in her bedroom. It was cool and

as dark as the rest of the house. It smells like her, he thought. Like sweet and spice and musk. The combination, the contradiction, that was Madi.

Despite the ready-made furnishings, she'd decorated the room in a way that said things about her she never would. The white eyelet quilt and pillow shams, the family photos in silver Victorian frames, the antique clock on the bedstand. And the big brown teddy bear on the bed, one that had obviously been well loved for many years.

Lance looked at her, and it was as if a key somewhere deep inside him turned and a door opened. Warmth rushed through him. With it came a strange sort of relief, a feeling of coming home. The urge to protect and cherish swelled in his chest. He drew her into his arms.

And held her. Quietly. Her heart beat against his, her breath whispered over his cheek. Even the air seemed gentled, the darkness softer than it had ever been. Just as he would be with her—softer, gentler.

With her in his arms he felt he had more to give, he felt he was the knight he'd always wanted to be—strong and good and . . . whole. The realization should have scared him; instead it made him happy.

"An old friend?" he whispered, indicating the teddy bear as he rubbed his cheek against her hair.

"That's Mr. B."

Her laugh contained a twinge of embarrassment. He imagined her blush.

"He's one of the few gifts I recall getting from my father. I was six."

"The year your parents divorced."

He'd remembered, she thought. Something so small shouldn't have the ability to warm her so, but it did. "Maybe he felt guilty. After that, he always sent a check."

Lance lowered his mouth to hers. She held nothing back. Her neck arched; she pressed her hands against his chest. Their tongues twined. How could this woman have so much sweetness? he wondered. She tasted of springtime and passion, of fall breezes and need. He found the pulse at her throat with his thumb. It strummed a strong, steady song.

When he ended the kiss, she sighed, then slowly opened her eyes. "You're wearing too few clothes."

He laughed. "How do you figure this is done, Hollywood?"

Her cheeks burned. "I know how it's done, but I would have liked to undress you. Slowly."

He nuzzled her mouth. "I wore this for you. I'd hoped to drive you crazy."

"You did." She slid her hands down his back, her fingers under the black elastic of his suit. "You're a wicked man, Lancelot Alexander." She inched the suit down, enjoying the heat of his skin—and his response. "I'm afraid you must pay for that wickedness."

With a laugh and a flick of his wrist, her skirt slipped to the floor. The suits were more difficult, more awkward. Finally nude, they sank to the bed.

For long moments they lay twined together, barely breathing. Madi drifted, feeling weightless, connected to Lance, not her own body any longer, but his as well. Her senses were swamped with him—the texture and scent of his skin, the crispness of the hair on his legs, the heat of his hands. And there were other things: the rustle of the sheets, the rhythmic song of the ocean that drifted in from outside, the moon's light, cool and white, as it fell over the bed.

The hardness between Lance's legs, the answering ache between hers.

They touched everywhere but moved not at all, and she was aroused to a pitch she hadn't thought possible. She knew Lance felt the same, for as they lay there his breathing became quicker, more labored.

She had expected passion, explosion. But this oneness, this calm, surprised her. Terrified her.

Would she ever feel so whole again?

She whimpered, and Lance moved, pinning her beneath him. He tangled his fingers in her hair; he caught her mouth. Madi trapped his tongue; she dug her nails into his shoulders.

He slipped into her without preamble but with infinite poetry. His moving inside her seemed as natural as the waves easing onto the shore, the sun dipping into the west.

She moved with him, holding him with arms and legs and mouth. She arched her back and gasped as sensations reverberated through her, as he stroked her until she thought she could bear no more.

The breath hissed from her lungs . . . A tremor, a tremble, a murmured word of satisfaction. His shudder, her plea, and together they rode the wave, then crested it.

Minutes passed. Madi wondered if her heart would ever slow its frenetic pace. But it did slow, and able to breathe once more, she pressed her mouth against his shoulder.

He rolled so that, still connected, they lay on their sides facing each other. He brushed the dampened tendrils of hair away from her face. "How do you feel?"

"Wonderful," she said simply.

He smiled. "I'm glad."

She nuzzled his neck. "How do you feel?"

"Wonderful."

"I'm glad too."

"You're an incredible woman, Madi Muldoon."

Laughter bubbled to her lips. "Just figured that out, did you? I must be pretty good in bed."

"No, you're great in bed, but that's not what I meant." He caught her laughter with his mouth. "How did you arrange to have that turtle haul itself out of the ocean to nest right in the middle of the gala?"

She grinned. "I told you I was good at my job. Besides, it wasn't the *middle* of the party. We would have missed her if not for the couple who had sneaked off to neck."

Lance arched an eyebrow. "Beautiful, talented, and modest too. My, my, some women have it all."

"That's me," she quipped, "Madi the modest." She rolled away from him. "Are you hungry? I could—"

He hauled her back. "Stop it, Madi. Stop being cute and glib and untouchable." He rubbed his thumb along her too stubborn jaw. "Tonight was about being honest. About being afraid and vulnerable and reaching out. You don't have to hide from me."

Don't I, Lancelot? She searched his face for long moments, then let him pull her into his arms and relaxed against him.

"I went to grade school with this kid named Rodney Willis," he murmured, softly stroking her back. "I used to call him Rodney the Rodent . . . but rat was more like it. He was one of those kids who was mean down to his bones. He made my life miserable until the sixth grade."

"What happened then?"

"I beat the hell out of him."

"Lance!"

She looked so shocked, he had to laugh. "Trust me, sweet, he had it coming. Anyway, I saw his name in the paper the other day."

"What did he do?"

"I was more interested in what he got—six to eight in the state pen." Lance began to move his fingers in small circles on her back. She sighed and yawned.

"Why are you telling me this?" She fought back another yawn. It sneaked out anyway.

"I'm not sure. Maybe because I felt so good . . . vindicated somehow . . . when I read that, maybe because I just needed to share it. He used to taunt me about being a bastard, tease me about my name. I always envied his having a real family. Deep down I guess I thought all the things he said about me were true. Of course I was too young to see something wasn't so perfect with his family or he wouldn't have become such a bully."

Madi tightened her arms around him, love swelling inside her until she thought she might burst. She could picture a miniature Lance, jaw clenched, spine stiff with pride and pain. She knew now why creating his perfect family was so important to him—he wanted in adulthood what had been denied him as a child.

"Thank you," she whispered.

"For what?"

For giving me yet another thing to love about you. "For trusting me enough to share that."

Lance gazed into her sleepy, satisfied eyes, a strange sensation settling in his chest. He hadn't shared that with anyone before, not even his mother. It had happened a long time ago; he'd told himself it didn't matter anymore. But it had mattered.

No more. Releasing the words, sharing his feelings with Madi, had somehow stolen the past's ability to wound.

But she'd yet to confide in him; she wasn't ready to trust.

At the truth of that, his smile faded. He kissed the top of her head. "Let's get some rest."

"Don't want to," she mumbled, curling closer into his side. Even as she completed the sentence, she was asleep.

The passion she'd expected earlier came later. As did the explosion. Lance awakened her with kisses in warm places, places soft with sleep, places that should have shocked her but didn't.

As if in a dream they tumbled together, growing bolder with every caress, wilder with each stroke of tongue or hand, until finally, exhausted and sated, they slept.

The next time Madi awoke, light glimmered on the horizon. Dawn, she thought, panicked. She wasn't ready for tomorrow, for it to be over. Not yet.

She slipped out of bed, careful not to disturb Lance, and crept through the house, pulling all the blinds, drawing the drapes. If she couldn't see the sun, the new day, it didn't exist. She could pretend for a little longer.

At the last moment she remembered the clocks and unplugged the one in the kitchen, dumped her bedside alarm in her sock drawer, and lastly, stuffed Lance's watch under the mattress.

Now, for a few more hours, she could believe in happy-ever-after.

This time it was she who awakened him with daring kisses and strokes meant to excite and ignite. They did, and with a cry of pleasure Madi made him hers.

Eight

His cheek tickled. Without opening his eyes, Lance swatted in the general direction of the itch. The tickle came again, this time accompanied by a muffled laugh, as feminine as it was mischievous. Madi was up to something.

Lance peeked at her through partially lowered lids. She lay propped up on an elbow watching him, her tawny gaze amused. Her glorious mane of hair was a riot of silky curls, her face was still soft with sleep. She was the most beautiful woman he'd ever known.

He smiled lazily and opened his eyes the rest of the way. "Well, don't you look like the cat that swallowed the canary."

She twirled a feather, obviously plucked from one of the pillows, between her fingers. "Don't I though?"

"And entirely too kissable."

She pouted playfully. "How can one be too kiss-able?"

He leaned over and caught her mouth. Her lips were warm and pliant and ready for his. A moment stretched into two, stretched into a dozen. He groaned and broke away from her. "That's how. You've worn me out, woman. If I don't get food and coffee—and quickly—I might die right here in this bed. It could be pretty embarrassing for you."

"And the Society." She trailed the feather across his beard-stubbled cheek. "I can see the headlines now: *Charity director dies of overexertion in fund-raiser's bed.* Say"—she widened her eyes—"that could be really good press. Think of the free publicity for the turtle—"

Lance hauled her to him. "I believe in giving to charities, but I have to draw the line somewhere."

She moved sinuously against him. "Draw it somewhere else, some other time." She fluttered her lashes. "Give till it hurts, Alexander."

He laughed and slapped her on the fanny, then pulled himself up, yawned, and stretched. "It already hurts, Hollywood."

Madi rolled onto her back. "I keep forgetting, you *are* an older man."

He sent her an arch look and sat up. "I wouldn't be so quick to judge. I don't see you doing jumping jacks."

Laughing, she followed him up. "Would you like to? Just name the number of rep—" She caught her breath as muscles not used to being worked screamed their protest.

"What were you about to say, whippersnapper?"

She groaned. "There's bound to be something

edible in the fridge . . . and some sort of muscle ointment in the medicine cabinet."

"I shouldn't take pity on you, but because I know how you got those sore muscles . . ." He smiled at her annoyed look. "Let's go out. We'll order more than an army could eat. I'll even pay." He looked at his wrist, frowned, then glanced at the bedside table. "What time is it anyway?"

"Time?" She leaned over and nipped his shoulder. "It doesn't exist. But I'll tell you this much, it's nowhere near morning."

He frowned. "Madi, isn't that the sun I see peeking in from behind the blinds?"

"Nope. It's the moon. A big, bright full moon."

"Okay, Hollywood, I'll bite. But I think it's only fair I know the rules of this little game we're playing."

"A smart boy like you should be able to figure them out."

He laughed and nuzzled her neck. "Where's my watch, witch?"

"Your watch is safe." She tipped her head and sighed as he moved his mouth to her ear. "Unless it's an obscenely expensive one, in which case I might just have to keep it."

"It's morning, Muldoon. And I want pancakes."

She caught his mouth in a brief kiss, then ducked out of his arms. In one fluid movement she was off the bed and into a silky robe. She wagged a finger at him. "Rule number one, Lance. It's not morning." She stopped at the door and looked teasingly over her shoulder at him. "Meet me in the kitchen in five."

Five minutes later Lance found her, bending as

she stared into the refrigerator. He glanced around the dim room, then back at her. After she'd left his arms and his brain had been able to clear, it hadn't taken him more than a moment to figure out what game they were playing. The night before she'd reached out to him—but only for the night. She'd promised him, but more importantly herself, that when the sun rose they would resume their old relationship.

She didn't understand that after the night they'd shared, they could never go back.

He leaned against the doorjamb, taking a moment to enjoy the way her aqua-colored robe caressed her curves. He remembered the way those curves had felt under his hands—like warmed silk—and cleared his suddenly dry throat. At this rate they would never have breakfast.

At the sound, Madi straightened and swung around. "I don't have the stuff to make pancakes. I have fruit."

"And we can't leave the house?"

"Or order out."

"Rule number two."

"And three."

He cocked his head. "Don't you find all this just a little dysfunctional, Madi?"

She sniffed. "Not at all. I call it manipulating my environment."

"You're your mother's daughter."

She stared at him a moment, obviously nonplussed by his comment. "What do you mean?"

"You told me your mother had a flair for both the dramatic and for manipulating the truth." He started toward her. "I think both are pretty appropriate here."

"Mmm, maybe you're right," she murmured. "But you know what?"

"What?"

She tipped her head back to meet his eyes. "I don't want to talk about my mother."

"No?"

"No." She placed her hands on his chest. "In fact, I don't want to talk at all."

So they didn't.

In the end, they feasted on fruit for breakfast. Luckily Madi had stopped at a stand Friday morning, and everything had looked so good, she'd bought more than she would have ever been able to eat on her own.

They fed each other the ripe, succulent fruit, the juices pooling on their lips and running down their fingers and hands. Later, they bathed each other, first with tongues, then with sponges, the scented water spilling over the sides of the tub with their passion.

Much later, when the light behind the closed blinds had changed again, making it really night, they lay on the living room floor, watching an old movie and eating popcorn laced with jalepeños.

"Why did you tell me about the two guys, Madi?"

She tilted her head back, surprised by his question. "Where did that come from?"

"I don't know." He ran his fingers through her hair.

"I never shared myself before." Even as the words

spilled out, a knot tightened in her stomach. She pushed the popcorn away and sat up. True and terrifying—she'd let Lance closer than any man had ever been. And still she wanted him closer.

"Max was a beach bum," she said finally, not looking at him. "He did some lifeguarding, but mostly he surfed. I liked him. He was fun."

Lance stroked her arm. "What happened?"

"Nothing, really. It ended. I didn't love him."

"And the other guy?"

"A performance artist. He was crazy. Irresponsible and daring." She laughed, the sound tinny to her own ears. "My mother hated him and all the other poets, artists, and surf bums I've dated. She's got this problem judging men only on their ability to take care of a woman's financial needs." Madi met his eyes. "What about the women in your past?"

"There weren't any." When she gazed at him with obvious skepticism, he laughed. "There were *women* but no relationships. I haven't had time."

"You've been too busy chasing the brass ring."

"Yes."

"My mother would like you. A lot."

"That wasn't fair."

Madi drew her knees to her chest. "I think it was."

Lance made a sound of frustration. "Nothing's wrong with working hard and wanting to take care of the people you love most, with wanting the best for your family."

"At the exclusion of the family? At the exclusion of emotional needs?"

"All successful men are not like your father."

"I never said that."

The edge in her voice was unmistakable. Lance knew he should tuck this argument away for another time, but he couldn't let it rest. "No, you live it instead."

"That's ridiculous." She leveled him with a frosty stare.

"Is it?" He faced her, just as evenly. "Your mother judges men on their earning ability. How do you judge men, Madi?"

"I don't judge them."

"That's bull. You judge them on how different they are from the men your mother married." She tried to get up but he grabbed her arm. "And more, you avoid relationships and keep people at arm's length because you're afraid of being hurt . . . the way the only man you ever loved hurt you."

She yanked her arm from his grasp. "I told you I never loved either of those guy—"

"Not 'those guys,' Madi. Your father."

His words were like a blow to her chest. Furious, she stood and faced him. "From construction work to psychoanalysis. That's quite a jump, Mr. Alexander. Perhaps you should consider getting a license before you practice."

He stood up too. "Prove I'm wrong."

"What?"

"See me again."

"You're crazy."

"No, this is crazy, Madi. This whole day. Pretending so we can be together. Making deals then side deals with yourself. Face the truth. We feel something for each other. When we touch, fires happen."

She took a step back, her heart thundering in her chest. "What are you suggesting?"

"That we don't deny it. That we continue seeing each other."

"We both have plans, we both know—"

"That hasn't changed. But my plans can be put on hold. There's no reason we can't continue what you outlined last night, no strings, no promises."

Disappointment left a bitter taste in her mouth. Worse was the realization that she'd hoped for more. Heat crept up her cheeks. What had she thought he'd been about to give her? she asked herself caustically. Some foolish declaration of undying love?

She narrowed her eyes. "'Seeing each other.' What a nice euphemism for sex."

This time it was he who narrowed his eyes. "What we shared was more than that, Madi. When two people reach out to each other, it's more than physical. But that's precisely what scares the hell out of you."

Dammit, he was right. She stiffened her spine. "But I don't need you now, Lance. I'm not reaching out."

He hauled her against him. "No, you're running."

"And what of you, Lance?" She balled her hands into fists against his chest. "You're manipulating even now. Working all the angles to get what you want. No romance. No hearts and flowers. No spontaneity. I'm surprised you don't have another one of your insipid tests for me to take. Or worse, if I said yes to this, you'd probably suggest we shake on it.

"I date the men I do because they're fun. They have time to play. They're not afraid to act crazy once in a while."

Her words struck a nerve. He told himself it was because he was tired, on edge. "I don't believe that," he said, his voice low, dangerous, "but you don't believe it either."

"What I believe," she shot back, "is no concern of yours. And I don't give a damn what you believe." She flattened her hands and pushed. "I think it's time you were going."

Lance stepped back. She wanted hearts and flowers, a little fun and craziness? Whether she realized it or not, she'd tossed down the gauntlet. And he never backed away from a challenge.

"Okay, Hollywood. It's your game and your rules." He crossed to the door, stopping and looking back at her when he reached it. "Count me in."

"What day is this?"

Madi looked down from her second-floor balcony to Lance's patio and scowled. Two weeks had passed since their argument and she had successfully avoided him—if she could consider two weeks of pure misery success. And now he was smiling up at her as if nothing had ever happened between them. He looked well-rested and sexy as hell. The rat. "As you no doubt already know," she answered, "it's Sunday."

"First day of the week, right?"

"To most people." She turned and started back inside. His next words stopped her.

"The Lancelot Heathcliff Alexander letter for the week is '*P*.'"

She whirled around. "What?"

He grinned. "I said, the Lancelot Heathcliff Alexander letter for the—"

"I heard you." She shook her head in frustration. "What does that mean?"

"You'll find out."

Laughing, he started back inside his condo.

"Lance, are you drunk?"

He stopped and smiled up at her. The curving of his lips was slow and suggestive, and Madi's breath caught. "Yeah, maybe I am. See you around, Muldoon."

Not if she could help it, he wouldn't. Madi stared at his now empty patio for a moment before slamming back into her own condo. Furious, she folded her arms across her chest. If he thought one ridiculous riddle was going to endear him to her or change her mind about him, he had another—

The doorbell interrupted her silent tirade. Promising herself she would pick up right where she left off, she went to answer it.

There was no one on her doorstep, only a basket of fruit. Squatting down, Madi examined the contents—a papaya, peaches, pears, and a pineapple. The note said: "Have a 'P'erfectly delightful breakfast. Lance."

She told herself she was not charmed. She told herself she knew what he was up to and that it simply would not work. A silly riddle accompanied by a delightful gift did not a new man make. And Lance Alexander was the wrong man for her.

By Saturday the things she told herself sounded

sillier than Lance's riddle. She looked around her now crowded little kitchen. All week the "P" gifts had kept coming. They'd ranged from the outrageously expensive—a thirty-inch strand of pearls on Wednesday—to the completely ridiculous—a thirty-gallon trash can filled with popcorn on Thursday evening.

Madi dragged a hand through her hair. There were five pounds of pistachio nuts, a furlined parka—Lord only knew what she would do with that one—a parrot puppet, a paisley-print scarf, and a pint of pink paint.

She was not weakening in her resolve. So what if the man was offering her fun and romance and spontaneity, just as she'd asked for? So what if she loved him so much it felt as if her heart might burst with hope each time the doorbell sounded or the phone rang? So what if she worried she couldn't live without him?

Which was precisely why she couldn't weaken in her resolve. Hadn't she seen, time and again, the carnage of marriage? Didn't she know that when it came to love, women made disastrous choices? Choices that killed their spirit and ate away their youth? Hadn't she promised herself she would never allow it to happen to her?

Yet here she was, so close to making the mistake of a lifetime she could almost taste it.

The doorbell didn't surprise her. Nor did the quick wish that Lance would be on the other side, or the acknowledgment that she was in deep trouble.

It wasn't Lance. The delivery boy held out a long florist's box. A moment later, she closed the door and stared at the box, drawing her eyebrows together. Not roses—unless of course, they were pink. Petunias? Pansies? Certainly not poinsettias.

She lifted the lid from the box and her stomach slid to her knees.

Peacock feathers. Six beautiful, shimmering peacock feathers.

Madi selected one and trailed it along her arm. It whispered sensuously over her skin, and she squeezed her eyes shut. He was mad. Wonderfully, delightfully insane. And she loved him. Totally and completely.

So why continue to deny it? Maybe Lance was right. They could have an affair. It didn't have to change either of their plans. At the end of the year she would go on to the Colorado Heart Foundation, and he could go on and start his storybook family.

No one would be hurt.

That lie was too outrageous even to pass by herself. Madi's eyes filled with tears. The truth was, she hurt now. She didn't think she could hurt anymore.

She had nothing else to lose. She'd already lost her heart.

The trip next door took less than a minute. When he didn't answer, she tried the door. It wasn't locked and she stepped inside. Music blared from his kitchen and she headed that way. "Lance, it's Madi. Lance?"

She found him singing along with the radio. He didn't have a bad voice, but he was a mess. There was flour in his hair, on his right cheek, his nose, and up to his elbows.

She fought back a laugh. Why did he have to be so darn irresistible? There ought to be a law about that, she decided. Then she wouldn't be in this stupid situation.

She folded her arms across her chest. "Mind telling me what you're doing?"

His head snapped up in surprise, then a lop-sided grin split his face. "Hi, Precious."

The laugh bubbled to the surface once more, and again she fought it back. "Lance, this *P* nonsense has to stop. No more presents. You hear me? No more."

"Aw, Precious." His smile became devilish. "You're not peeved are you?"

"That's it! I want you to promise me there'll be no more *P* gifts and no more *P* words. Is that"—she couldn't help herself—"perfectly clear?"

Lance shrugged and started slicing mushrooms. "Your loss."

Madi told herself not to ask. She told herself he was manipulating her—again. She asked anyway. "Why's it my loss?"

"Nevermind." He didn't look up from the mushrooms. "You made yourself clear. If you don't mind letting yourself out . . ."

She did mind. For the last week he'd been darn creative in an attempt to get her to talk to him. Now here she was . . . and playing second fiddle to fungus. "You're not going to make this easy, are you?"

He looked up at that. "Turnabout's fair play."

She let her breath out in an annoyed huff. He

was right again. "Okay. We can continue seeing each other. No strings, no promises. Just like you wanted the other night."

"Not good enough, Hollywood. Now I want some hearts and flowers." He met her eyes evenly. "And I don't want to shake hands on the deal."

A trembling started deep inside her. Already this was more complicated than she'd told herself it would be. Already she wanted to promise him everything. She struggled to keep the tremor out of her voice.

"I . . . want you, Lance. It's not a deal. It's not just . . . sex. It's you and me and the way we make each other feel." Her voice broke. "I've been miserable since our fight."

Lance tossed down his paring knife and strode over to her. He cupped her face in his hands, and the yeasty smell of the flour filled her head. She wondered if she would ever be able to bake again and not think of Lance and this night.

"If you have anything else to say, Madi, say it now. Because in a moment I'm going to kiss you until you're too weak to talk."

"A moment's too long to wait," she whispered, pulling his head down to hers.

His lips were warm, already parted. She held him to her, reveling in the taste and the texture that was Lance.

And the scent. She pulled away, just a fraction. Kissing him reminded her of a dive of an Italian restaurant located on the outskirts of L.A. Smiling, she nuzzled his jaw. "Lance?"

"Hmm . . ." He trailed his hands down her back until he found and cupped her buttocks.

His arousal was all too evident. Her own desire washed over and through her. When she spoke, the words came out a breathless whisper. "What was my *P* gift going to be?"

He nipped at her bottom lip. "I thought you said—"

"Forget what I said."

"Pizza," he whispered.

She laughed, arching her neck as he found her pulse point and plundered it. "I take it back. I want my present."

"Uh-uh." He swung her into his arms and carried her from the kitchen to the bedroom. "I have another, better gift for you." He kicked the bedroom door shut behind them. "Passion."

Nine

Lance had given her yet another "P" gift.

Pregnancy.

Madi stared at herself in the mirror, placing her hands tentatively against her abdomen. It couldn't be true. But it was. Madison Muldoon, thirty years old and unmarried, was six weeks pregnant.

She turned to the side, examining her reflection. Her body didn't look any different. But it felt different; she felt different. Lusher, more womanly. Good Lord, she felt sexy. Who would have thought it possible? Every other woman she'd known had felt sick and shaky during her first trimester, and here she was, wishing Lance was stroking her and murmuring the kind of words excited, expectant fathers did.

Lance.

Her legs began to tremble, and she crossed to the bed and sat down. The last four weeks had been wonderful. They'd talked and laughed and made love. They'd gone on turtle patrols and walks on the beach, they'd worked with her volunteers on the fall event. He'd even taught her about the construction business.

By mutual, unspoken agreement, though, they'd never discussed their relationship or the future.

Because they had both decided they had neither, not together.

She dropped her head into her hands. But now the future—her future—was here. She couldn't evade or avoid or pretend; she had decisions to make. She had to tell him.

But how was she going to do it?

Overwhelmed, Madi flopped back on the bed. She'd better decide, and fast. Lance would be there any minute.

She squeezed her eyes shut. She needed more time. She needed quiet, space. . . . She needed Lance's arms around her.

A sob caught in her throat, and she fought it back. Now wasn't the time for tears, she told herself, digging her fingernails into her palms. After Lance had come and gone she could fall apart. For now she had to be strong.

She uncurled her fingers and laid her hands gently over her still-flat stomach. Although a part of her screamed for her to skip town without telling him, she knew she couldn't do that. It wouldn't be fair, wouldn't be right. She wasn't a coward.

So, she would just tell him, flat out.

And he would say . . . what? She frowned. What did she want him to say? An hysterical laugh bubbled to her lips. She wanted him to promise undying love and happily-ever-after. She wanted the impossible.

Madi pulled herself into a sitting position and swiped at the tears on her cheeks. There was a baby inside her. Her baby. A new life. She touched her belly again, a smile pulling at the corners of her mouth. Hadn't she been longing for a child? To be a mother? Hadn't her desire never to marry been the only thing holding her back? She'd thought she would never be able to have this experience, this joy.

She laughed. She could do this. She was independent, she had money saved and a marketable skill. Despite this ridiculous incident, she was responsible, mature.

Now she could have it all.

Just as quickly as it had begun, her laughter died. No, not all. She wouldn't have Lance. She would never know the feeling of loving and being loved in return. She would never experience the joy of a man and woman—mother and father—sharing the moment when their child took its first steps or said its first word.

The tears were back, and again she strove to ignore them. Even if she could bring herself to believe in happily-ever-after, even if she could convince herself to give marriage a try, she couldn't with Lance. He didn't believe in love. He'd told her so.

The bell rang, announcing his arrival. She stood, smoothed her white T-shirt dress, and ran her fingers through her hair. She could have used more time to splash cold water on her face or put on a little blush. She hadn't any time left.

She took one last glance in the mirror. Her baby—their baby—deserved more than a workaholic father who was never around. He or she deserved more than an unhappy mother and being part of a marriage of convenience.

Squaring her shoulders, Madi started for the door as he rang again. She would tell Lance about the baby, then she would tell him good-bye.

Resolutions made to the cool reflection in her bedroom mirror evaporated as she swung open her front door. He'd brought her flowers. Little purple ones that looked velvety and smelled like heaven. She buried her nose in the bouquet, wishing he'd taken the time to change, wishing his smile wasn't so sleepy, his hair so tousled. She smiled weakly and stepped aside so he could come in.

She watched as he shrugged out of his jacket, then began loosening his tie. He looked great in gray. It brought out the silver of his hair, the green of his eyes. She once thought his choice in suits and colors conservative to the point of being fuddy-duddy, yet now she saw them as strong and solid and even. A reflection of the man himself.

"Madi?"

She blinked. "I'm sorry, what?"

"I asked, how was your day?"

She stared at him, horrified. *Had he found out already? Had someone seen her at the doctor's office?* She cleared her throat. "What do you mean?"

"I mean, did you have a good day? You know, like everything went well, no major problems or petty annoyances." He laughed. "You're kind of jumpy tonight. Something must have happened."

"No, nothing happened. Everything's fine. It's only that . . ." She searched for something reasonable to say. "It's only that you haven't kissed me yet."

"Is that all?" He drew her to him, then caught her mouth in a searing kiss.

She melted against him. *Would this be the last time he kissed her like this?* Desperation curled through her, and she held onto him, deepening the kiss as he made a move to end it. When it did end, she rested her forehead against his chest, her heart thundering, her breath coming in small gasps.

Lance's laugh was husky. "I could come home to that every night. You must have missed me today."

She took a step back, trembling from the tips of her fingers to her toes. "I'm going to put these in water. Be right back."

Turning, she fled to the kitchen. Good Lord, at this rate he'd have her committed before she even had the chance to tell him. She drew in a deep, steadying breath as she filled a vase with water. Calm, she told herself. Cool and in control.

"I think it's full."

She jumped as first she realized he'd followed her, and second that water was spewing out of the top of the vase. "So it is," she murmured, shutting off the tap. "I must have been . . . thinking . . . about something."

He crossed the room and wrapped his arms around her. "This may be indelicate and none of my business, but is it your time of the month?"

This was her opportunity, she told herself. A perfect lead-in.

She opened her mouth and . . . croaked. She tried again, and again her throat closed over the words. All that emerged was mangled air.

"I wouldn't have figured you for the type who was easily embarrassed," he murmured, rubbing his chin against the top of her head. "But then, I learn something new about you every day."

And today's lesson will be a doozie, she thought. *Well, Lance, you see, I ovulate twice a month. I guess you could call me a fertile turtle.*

A hysterical giggle rose in her throat; she swallowed it. "Have you eaten?"

"Uh-huh." He nibbled at the side of her neck. "Old man Dickerson and I broke bread." She heard the smile in his voice. "He even insisted on picking up the check. He is very pleased with the progress of his new complex."

She turned in his arms, thoughts of babies and goody-byes momentarily evaporating. "Oh, Lance, I'm so happy for you."

"Me too." He rubbed his nose playfully against hers. "But then I have a lot to be happy about these days."

Her stomach took a nosedive. Would he still be able to say that by the end of the evening? "Lance, I—"

"Dance with me, Madi." He drew her out of the kitchen and toward the stereo in the living room.

She resisted. "No, Lance, we have to talk—"

"You talk too much."

"This is serious."

"So's this." He flipped a switch, and a slow,

bluesey tune filled the room. "Before I met you, I didn't like to dance. I found it frivolous and a chore and a good reason to avoid weddings."

He pulled her against his chest and began to sway to the music. "But I want to dance with you. I want to hold you close and move real slow." He tangled his fingers in her hair. "And while we're pressed together, your heart beating wildly against mine, I want to whisper erotic, outrageous promises in your ear."

Her legs turned to marshmallow, and she clung to him. Cursing her own weakness, she tipped her face up to his. "And then?"

"And then . . ." He swung her around, bending her slightly over his arm. "I want to keep each and every one of those promises."

Madi squeezed her eyes shut, dizzy with need. Would it be so wrong to hold onto the truth for a little longer? Would it be so wrong to be with him this one last time?

"Tell me," she whispered, her voice husky with her own wanting, "what you're going to do."

"I can do better than that, Hollywood." He lowered his mouth until it hovered only a fraction from hers. "I'll show you."

He did just that.

Much later, Madi slipped out of bed and began to dress. From behind her she heard Lance's sigh.

"I guess that means it's time for us to get to work."

"Work?"

"You said you wanted my input on the scavenger hunt."

She'd completely forgotten! Madi shook her head

as she knotted the drawstring waist of her gray sweats. "Right. The file's on the kitchen counter."

"What's wrong, Madi?" She glanced back at him. "You're not yourself tonight."

"We have to talk," she said, fighting the urge to look away. "But not here."

"Why not?" he asked softly. "We communicate pretty well right here."

"No." She shook her head, one hand instinctively covering her abdomen. "I think you'll be happier if we don't. I'll make coffee." She turned and fled the room.

The light in the kitchen was bright, even harsh. It was the kind of light that didn't smooth or soften, the kind of light for candid conversations. For good-byes.

Madi took two mugs from the cupboard. She'd made the coffee strong, remembering at the last moment that she shouldn't have anything but decaf now.

She offered Lance a cup. He declined.

They faced each other. He looked on edge, looked like a man spoiling for a fight. She swallowed hard. She'd already handled this all wrong.

"Well?" he prompted, folding his arms across his chest.

"Well . . ." She wiped her damp palms against her thighs. "I'm not sure where to begin."

"So just begin."

How like him, she thought, almost wildly. No nonsense, cut right to the chase, Lancelot Alexander. She almost wished she didn't know him so well.

And as he was so often, he was right. Drawing in

a deep breath, she took his advice. "I never wanted to be a mother, never wanted children. I never even particularly cared for them. It wasn't that I disliked them, I thought they were cute and all . . . but I just thought I didn't have the maternal instinct. And then Tina had Morgan."

Madi crossed to the sliding glass doors and stared out at the ocean. Tonight the moon was barely a crescent. As a result, the beach was dark, the water darker still.

Without turning, she continued. "Have you ever held a newborn, Lance? They're so soft and small . . . they smell so good." She laughed, her eyes brimming with tears. "They have these ten little toes, and these ten little fingers." She swung back around and held out her own hands. "Their fingernails are perfectly shaped but so delicate, they're translucent."

Lance hadn't moved. He'd followed her with his eyes, but his stance hadn't changed. There was a stillness about him, as if he were tuning in to her every nuance; a watchfulness, as if he sensed danger but wasn't sure of its source.

She drew a shuddering breath. "All of a sudden I had these strange, new feelings . . . these yearnings. I began having trouble sleeping. I began questioning my choices and fighting this vague dissatisfaction with everything in my life." She clasped her hands in front of her. "I denied the truth for a while, I fought it. But the truth was, I ached for what I thought I would never want. I ached for a baby."

"What are you telling me, Madi?"

"I'm going to be a mother, Lance."

He didn't move. He didn't make a sound. His expression was one of total shock, total disbelief.

The tears she'd been fighting spilled over, and she turned away from him. "I didn't get pregnant on purpose. You have to believe that. In fact, at first I was shocked. And scared." She turned back to him, not caring that he would see her tears. "But now I'm delighted. I didn't think I would have this opportunity, Lance. I thought this was an experience I would go through life without. I hope you can be happy about this too."

"You're pregnant." He shook his head. "You're telling me you're going to have a baby. My baby."

"Yes."

"How did this happen?"

She smiled, remembering how the doctor had looked at her when she'd voiced the same question. "Apparently, I ovulate twice a month. The doctor said it's not as uncommon as one would think." Her cheeks heated. "I've never had a problem because I've never . . . well, you know, slept around, and . . . I've never been with anyone as long, or a much, as you."

Lance cleared his throat, his expression still dazed. "I'm not certain exactly what you're getting at."

Hurt cannonballed into her. He couldn't even pretend to be pleased. She stiffened her spine. "I don't want anything from you, if that's what you're worried about. I wouldn't have even told you, only I thought you had the right to know." She inched her chin up a little more. "I can do this on my own. I *want* to do this on my own."

"So, you're saying I have a right to know, but

nothing else?" He stared hard at her. "I'm the father. I have a say in this."

"No." She shook her head. "I'm going to have this baby, Lance. And I'm not going to give it up for adoption. I can give it a good, loving home. Any number of charities would hire me full time. It's only a matter of deciding where I want to live. I thought being close to Tina would be good. That way the baby will have family nearby and—"

"We'll get married."

"What?" It was Madi's turn to look dazed.

"We'll get married. Right away."

"No."

He didn't listen, but started going through drawers until he found a phone book. "I have a friend who's a judge—"

"No."

He looked at her then. "You don't understand what you're getting yourself into. Raising a child with two parents is hard. With one it's—"

"I understand what I'm getting into. I want this baby, Lance. I don't care about the dirty diapers or three o'clock feedings. I'm not a damsel in distress. You don't have to charge in and save the day. I'm happier than I've been in years."

He crossed to her in three strides. He didn't touch her, although he was so close she could see the anger in his eyes, the muscle that jumped in his jaw. "I was a bastard, Madi. I won't have that for my child."

Her heart began to thump uncomfortably. Why hadn't she thought of that? It was so obvious. She struggled to control both her breathing and her panic. "Times have changed, Lance. There's no longer a stigma attached to a child without a father. I'd wager that fifty percent of the children today have nontraditional families—"

"I want this baby."

Her breath caught, her heart broke. If only he'd said he wanted her with such conviction. "I won't marry you."

He caught her upper arms. "This child is mine. I have rights."

The panic she'd tried to control curled through her. Why hadn't she skipped town when she'd had the chance? How had she been so foolish to think this would be at least relatively easy?

"Lance, you'll have other"—she almost couldn't say the words—"other children. You're going to find the woman you want to marry, the woman who fits into your plans. I flunked your test, remember?"

"Plans can change. They have to change." He stroked his hands up her arms to her shoulders. He lowered his voice. "I've changed, Madi."

Had he? He moved his fingers in slow, soothing circles, easing the tight muscles in her shoulders and neck. It would be so easy just to give in and say yes, just give in and let him take care of everything.

Just as her mother had always done.

"No." Madi shook her head, taking a step back, away from his touch. "I can't."

He followed her. "You're afraid, Madi. Don't be. It's the perfect solution, the logical solution. Why do this alone when you can have help? Think about it for a moment and you'll see I'm right."

She flipped the lock on the sliding glass doors

and stepped out onto the second-story deck. The darkness swallowed her; the sound of the ocean enveloped her. She turned back to Lance. He stood in the doorway, a strong dark silhouette in the rectangle of light.

She drew in a deep, unsteady breath. "No, Lance, it wouldn't work."

"What would it take to convince you?" he asked softly, stepping out of the light, toward her. "What can I do to get you to say yes?"

Madi squeezed her eyes shut. If he loved her, she would take the chance. *Swallow your pride, Madi Muldoon, and tell him. What do you have to lose?*

She opened her eyes and met his. "If—" Her throat closed over the words. She tried again, gasping in air, feeling as if her heart would burst from fear. "If you said . . . you loved me. If you said it and . . . meant it, then maybe I could . . . I would . . ."

This time it was Lance who turned away. Seconds became minutes. When he finally spoke, his tone was harsh. "Ask me something else, Madi. Anything else."

The sound of pain was hers, low and wrenched from her. She wrapped her arms around herself and fought back another moan. It seemed she'd had more to lose than she'd thought.

"I'm incapable of the kind of love you ask for. I don't believe in it . . . can't believe in it." He turned back to her and caught her hands. "Try to understand, Madi, I never saw anything good come of love."

She stared blankly at their joined hands, then lifted her gaze to his. "Or I of marriage."

Lance swore and tightened his fingers on hers. "I believe in commitment. I believe in family, in give-and-take between partners, in the kind of love that respects and nurtures. I'll be a good husband, Madi, a good father. I want this baby."

He brought her hands to his lips, kissing first one, then the other. "We get along well, Madison. In the bedroom and out. You could continue on at the Society, continue helping the turtles. You like Melbourne Beach. It would be a good place to raise our child."

She wanted to say yes. She wanted to throw herself into his arms and let herself lean on him. He would make sure everything was all right. And if she believed that, she was her mother's daughter after all.

She slipped her hands from his. He would never love her as she needed to be loved. "We would end up at each other's throats. Soon, you wouldn't want to touch me, or I you. I want more for my baby—"

"Our baby."

"—than two people who only tolerate each other, two people consumed with regrets."

Silence stretched between them. Finally, softly, Lance said, "We can do this easy, or we can do this messy. I have rights. I'll take you to court if I have to. I'll get partial custody. I can get a court order so you can't leave the state."

"You wouldn't!"

"Try me."

He was as hard, as manipulative as she'd first thought him. Even now he was working the angles, making deals. She couldn't marry a man like that. She wouldn't.

"Don't do this, Lance."

"You've left me no choice. What's it going to be, Madi?"

Heart breaking, she held her head high and met his determined gaze with her own. "I guess I'll see you in court."

Ten

He'd lied to her. He'd lied to himself.

She would never believe he loved her now.

Lance stared moodily out at the deserted beach. Though it was barely evening, the sky was dark, the swirling black clouds heavy with the threat of rain.

He threw open his sliding glass doors and stepped out onto his deck. The wind's fury hit him full in the face; he didn't back down or turn away. A storm of this magnitude always spelled trouble for the turtles. The rising water would wipe out many nests, and much of the debris that washed up onto the beach was dangerous to the nesting females. But those kinds of hazards were out of his hands. The turtles had been battling Mother Nature for millions of years, and doing quite well until man had come along and started mucking things up.

Lance rested his hands on the deck-railing and

leaned into the wind. It seemed his own fate had been taken out of his hands as well. He'd fallen in love with Madi without his own consent, going against everything he believed to be right for him.

He let out a long, frustrated sigh. He'd been fooling himself so long, he didn't even know when it had happened. Had it been that first morning when she'd bested him? Or that first time their lips had met and he'd tasted the vulnerable girl beneath the cocky woman?

He laughed, the sound hard and tight against the wind. The truth was, it didn't matter when it happened or how. The deed was done—he was scared silly, head-over-heels in love with her. Everything about her: her strengths and her fears, her wit and her evasions, all the things that made Madison Muldoon the most fascinating woman he'd ever known.

A particularly fierce gust of wind slammed into him, and he tightened his grip on the railing. What an idiot he'd been. All that stuff about just seeing her, no strings and no promises, that had been a lot of bull. And the stuff about his plans to resume finding a wife after their affair had run its course. That had been nothing more than hot air.

But the worst had been the bit about marrying her only to give the baby a name—that had been self-preservation, pure and simple.

Even though he'd been terrified and tense and aching as he'd proposed to her, he'd still been too blind—or too hardheaded—to see the truth. He'd done such a good job of convincing, he'd even convinced himself.

Madi would never believe him now. What would he do if he'd lost her?

Even as panic slugged him in the gut, Lance straightened, angry at himself. He wasn't a quitter. He was a man of action, a man accustomed to shaping his own destiny. There had to be a way to convince Madi that he loved her, the whole woman, not just her ability to make babies or be a wife and partner.

And that now, he believed in love.

But how? He'd never considered himself a romantic man. It had taken all his creativity to come up with that "P" thing. Even then he'd cheated. He'd remembered his mother telling him about a romance she'd just read, effusively describing the grand romantic gestures the hero had made to win his lady's love. Lance laughed without humor. And then Darnell Peabody had called. He'd put two and two together and had started shopping.

Lightning flashed across the sky, thunder following. The storm was almost on top of him, yet Lance didn't make a move to go inside. He faced the turbulent ocean, scowling. What would one of his mother's romantic heroes do now? He'd been weaned on the classic—and not so classic—romances, but for the life of him the only hero he could think of was his namesake.

That he was even trying to put himself in the head of a centuries' old legend said something, and it wasn't good news. He'd sunk to the level of lovesick fool, a man besotted.

He should just march next door, explain the facts, and insist she marry him.

Lance groaned. It would never work. She'd toss

him out on his ear. He dragged his hands through his hair once more. So, what *would* Lancelot, favored knight of the Round Table, do?

Sweep her into his arms and carry her off into the sunset.

The first of the rain hit Lance's cheek even as he narrowed his eyes in thought.

Light glimmered on the horizon, not quite dawn. Madi let herself out of her condo and headed down to the beach. The air still smelled like the storm, she thought. Like the sea and the sky and things that thrived on both. And it smelled fresh and cleansed, like a new day.

She ran a hand wearily across her forehead. She wished she could feel so fresh, so new and full of hope. She hadn't been able to sleep, and although she would like to blame the storm that had raged well into the night, she couldn't.

The truth was, she'd been unable to sleep for wanting Lance.

She kicked at a piece of driftwood washed up with the storm. The beach was a mess, littered with shells and driftwood and all manner of sealife, and also, sadly, with things that had nothing to do with nature and everything to do with man's lack of respect for it.

She sighed and stepped around a piece of a tire. Later she would bring out some trash bags and do what she could to clean up.

If only she could clean up the mess of her life so easily. Spending her days and nights crying wasn't good for her. It wasn't good for the baby. And in the week since she'd refused Lance's proposal, she'd been depressed and weepy and sick as a dog.

But worse, much worse, she'd been wavering in her decision. Madi shoved her hands into her pockets. Even though she knew it would be absolutely the wrong thing to do, she'd considered settling for less, settling for a marriage of convenience with a man who would never love her.

She had to leave. That realization had hit her in the middle of the night, at the peak of the storm. Although she'd grown to love this place, being close to Lance was killing her. She would give her notice at the Society and go back to California.

Pain ripped through her at the thought, and she steeled herself against it. She knew of no other alternative. Putting geographical distance between herself and Lance was the only way she knew to put some emotional distance between them.

Aching, Madi folded her arms across her chest. Lance would forget about her. Of that she was certain. She was less certain that he would forget the baby or his promise to sue for partial custody.

Sighing again, she scanned the beach. A large bundle of trash, what looked like a fisherman's nets tangled with all manner of other things, lay ahead of her.

She walked toward it, shaking her head. Maybe there was someone she could call to haul this away. It was too large and heavy for her to do much wi—

Madi stopped in her tracks, not believing what she thought she saw. It looked as if there was a turtle tangled in the net.

She ran then, covering the remaining distance in seconds. Her breath caught. Her eyes hadn't deceived her—one of the mama turtles was trapped in the net.

Heart thundering in her chest, Madi knelt down and gently moved aside some seaweed, trying to ascertain if the turtle was still alive.

How could she tell? Madi frowned. The turtle's eyes were closed, but something about her seemed alive, not dead. But still . . . Hands shaking, she tried carefully to untangle the net from around the creature. After several minutes and almost no headway, she knew the truth. She couldn't do this alone.

Lance would know what to do. She had to get Lance. She stood and looked back the way she'd come, then shifted her gaze back to the turtle. Even in the time she'd been standing there deciding what to do, the sun had climbed into the sky. She might not have much time.

"Hang on," she murmured, gently touching the reptile's shell. "I'll get help. Just please, please hang on."

She turned and started back toward the condos at a dead run.

Madi had no idea how long it took her to reach Lance's or how long she waited for him to answer her pounding. She only knew relief as he opened the door and pulled her into his arms.

"My, God, Madi, what's wrong?"

Panting for breath, all she could do was look at him. His panic registered, but as much as she wanted to reassure him she was all right, she couldn't catch her breath.

"No, don't answer." He lifted her and carried her to his couch, laying her gently on it. "I'll call your doctor. Wait, I don't know who your . . . Nevermind, I'll call my doc . . . No, maybe I should call an ambu—"

She shook her head, clutching at his sleeve. "Lance . . . need . . . help, down on the—"

"Tell me where it hurts, sweetheart." He ran his trembling hands over her damp forehead, then down her arms as if assuring himself nothing was broken. "Is it the baby? Is it—"

She grabbed his hands. "On the beach . . ." She paused, struggling for air.

His expression went from concern to murderous. He dropped to his knees next to the couch. "Did someone hurt you? Did someone try to—"

"No, a turtle . . . the storm washed up one of the mamas and . . ." Madi drew in a deep, almost steady breath and started again. "I'm okay," she managed. "The storm washed up a fisherman's net and a turtle . . . is trapped—"

Lance understood then. He jumped up and ran to the phone. "How did she look?" he asked, dialing. "Was she still alive?"

Hysteria bubbled up inside her, and Madi fought it back. "I don't know. I think she's alive, but I couldn't tell for sure."

He held up a hand. "Hal, we've got a mama tangled in nets down here by me. Send the rescue squad A.S.A.P. And call Sea World. Madi found her and she isn't sure what shape she's in. She could have drowned out at sea trapped in that net."

"Drowned!" Madi shot up into a sitting position, then held her head as dizziness overtook her.

Without saying good-bye, Lance slammed down the receiver and raced back to her. "I'm calling the doctor—"

"Don't worry about me, I'm just a little di—"

"Don't worry about you? When I saw you standing there like that . . . Dammit, Madi, I thought—" He dragged his hands through his hair, and Madi saw they were shaking. "We'll talk about what I thought later. For now . . . " He eased her back into a reclining position. "Stay put, you hear me! You've seen enough action for today."

"But the turtle—"

"She's not in a lot of danger on the beach, not yet anyway." He arranged several of the sofa pillows behind her. "The nets could harm her, depending how hard and long she struggled against them. The biggest worry is that she got trapped underwater . . ."

He let his voice trail off, but the words hung between them nonetheless. *And couldn't come up for air.* "There's nothing you can do for her now. But if you so much as move from this couch, you're going to have to answer to me. Got it?"

He was trying to look stern. He looked terrified instead. Warmth spread through her. "Yes, Lance."

"I've got to go. You'll stay put?"

He loved her. He didn't realize it yet, but he loved her. She smiled. "Yes, Lance."

He leaned down and brushed his lips across hers. "I've got to go."

"Go."

With one last worried look at her, he slammed out the door.

Madi pulled herself into a sitting position, euphoria replacing dizziness. She stared at the closed door. He loved her. He really did. Now all she had to do was figure out a way to make him realize it.

Two and a half hours later, Lance let himself back into his condo. The turtle had been alive, but was both seriously dehydrated and in shock. The people from Sea World had taken her, and although Lance knew she would get the best care possible and that her recovery was out of his hands, he couldn't help worrying.

He paused in the entryway, running his fingers through his hair, drawing in a deep breath. This wasn't how he'd planned to approach Madi, wasn't how he'd planned to tell her he loved her. But the opportunity had presented itself, and only a foolish man let opportunities slip by.

He stepped into the living room, and disappointment hit him like a major leaguer's fast ball. The couch was empty; she was gone.

He searched the condo, hoping like the lovesick fool he was that he would find her in the shower or napping on the bed. When he proved what he already knew—that the condo was empty—he searched again, this time for a note.

There was nothing.

Lance sank onto the edge of the bed. Things were as bad as he'd feared. There was nothing left for him to do but put his plan into motion.

Madi stopped in front of her sliding glass doors, not believing her eyes. She blinked once, then twice. The apparition didn't change. Crossing the boardwalk from the beach was a knight on a white steed.

Heart thundering in her chest, she threw open the glass doors and ran out onto the deck. The knight rode bareback, his only armor a helmet topped with a brilliant blue and gold plume, and a lance whose pennon of the same colors fluttered in the breeze. He held himself awkwardly, as if he were unused to riding and more than a bit uncomfortable.

Love ballooned inside her until she thought she might burst with it. She wasn't a damsel in distress, but he *was* her knight in shining armor. How could she ever have thought him a man without romance?

She leaned out over the railing.

Lance flipped up his visor. "Lady Madison."

"Sir Lancelot," she returned just as seriously.

"I've come to carry you off into the sunset."

"Have you?"

"Yes."

"And if I refuse to come?"

He would die. Lance said instead, "I'll sling you over my shoulder and take you anyway." He frowned. "Dammit, Madison, I love you."

She laughed down at him, her heart soaring with joy. And disbelief. "You're mixing your romantic heroes. I think I heard a little of Rhett Butler in that."

"Dammit, Madi—"

"You said that before." She pushed her hair behind her ear; it immediately tumbled back over her shoulder. "Where's the rest of your armor?"

He scowled, yanked off his helmet, and dropped it to the ground. "I love you, Madi Muldoon. I was an idiot and a fool not to see it before. I'm prepared to do anything it takes to make you believe—"

"I believe you," she said quietly.

He stared up at her. "You do?"

"And I love you, Lancelot Heathcliff Alexander."

"You do?"

"Yes. I'm accepting your proposal of marriage."

"You are?"

"That's right, so don't you dare try to weasel out of it."

Lance shuddered with relief. She loved him. She was going to marry him. He could breathe now. "Never," he said, smiling. "But I thought I'd have to do a lot more convincing."

Madi gazed down at him, letting all the love she felt shine from her eyes. "I knew you loved me this morning. I didn't think you'd realized it, but I did. You were terrified that something had happened to me, Lance. Not the baby, not first anyway. I could see in your eyes that you thought you'd lost me."

"Are you telling me I can get off this beast now and come insi—"

"Not a chance, buster. You're my knight in shining armor and you're carrying me off into the sunset." Laughing, she whirled around, then tossed over her shoulder, "Don't you move, I'll be right out."

A small crowd had gathered, and as Madi mounted the horse, they burst into applause. As her and Lance's lips met, they roared their approval.

"You're blushing again," she whispered against his mouth.

"I'm a forty-year-old conservative, no-nonsense businessman, Madi. This would have been embarrassing without the crowd. Right now I feel like crawling under a rock for, oh . . . about ten years."

She hugged him hard. "You can't fool me, not anymore. You're a dyed-in-the-wool, hopeless romantic. Your mother would be proud."

"Yeah, I guess she would." He kissed her again. "Ready, Lady Madison?"

She was, and they started down the beach just as the sun dipped below the horizon and the sky transformed into a brilliant palette of fiery hues.

Much later as they lay naked under the sheets, Madi sighed and looked up at him. "We need to talk."

Lance trailed his fingers across her shoulder. "As long as you haven't changed your mind about loving me."

"I'll never change my mind about that." She paused, pressing her face against his chest and breathing in the smell that was all-male and all Lance. "I want to talk about my mother."

"Your mother?"

"Mmm. I've realized some things in the last few days, things I should have realized years ago." She snuggled closer to his side. "I always saw my mother as a sort of victim of her sex. I saw marriage as this huge trap, this prison. I realize now, those were only my own rationalizations for my mother's behavior. She and the other women I know made their own choices, whether I thought them bad ones or not."

She moved her hands up his chest to his shoulders. "My mother never married for love. She married for money and security and prestige. And she always got what she went into the union wanting." Madi met his eyes. "For myself, I'm marrying for love. Not for a father for this baby, not for security or anything else. For love."

Lance cupped her face in his palms. "I won't let you down, Madi Muldoon." He brought his mouth to hers in a deep, stirring kiss. When he ended it they were both short of breath. "I've realized some things too. You were right when you accused me of using my 'wife plan' to protect myself from pain. The decisions I kept insisting were made from cool-headed logic were anything but. I was terrified of being hurt, like my mother had been hurt . . . like I'd been hurt as a child."

"Oh, Lance—"

He gently laid his fingers over her mouth. "There's more. I also realized I was angry at my mother, for not being able to give up her romantic illusions and marry another man, for not giving me the family I yearned for. Because I adored her, I turned that anger on love."

"That's all behind us now."

"Yes." He combed his hands through her hair, knowing he would never tire of feeling it against his skin. "That first night on the beach," he asked softly, "when you made a wish on the full moon, what did you wish for?"

She laughed. "I felt like a fool because I wished

for what I was certain didn't exist, what I'd almost convinced myself I didn't want."

"And that was?"

"Someone to love me for myself. The kind of relationship I'd read about but thought was only fiction. A child to fill my arms . . . and my heart."

His breath caught; he tightened his arms. "I plan to devote the next forty or fifty years making sure your wish comes true."

"It already has."

He laughed. "So, your mother was right about full moons."

"As was yours, about love." Madi smiled and shifted so she straddled him. "I like this mothers being right stuff. After all, I'm going to be one soon and I've always preferred being right."

Lance laced his fingers with hers. "Why do I have the feeling I'm in way over my head?"

"Because"—she sank slowly onto him—"you are."

Epilogue

The breeze off the ocean was mild, comforting even as it stroked Lance's skin. He squinted against the brilliant sunlight as he watched the golden-haired girl frolic in the surf. She was breath-catchingly beautiful, and had captured his heart as surely as her mother had.

He smiled and waved as the girl called to him, then raced toward him, a bundle of energy wearing a fluorescent-pink bathing suit.

She stopped in front of him and solemnly handed him a small but perfect seashell. "Happy birthday, Daddy."

A tightness in his chest, he gazed up at her. "You must have looked very hard to find one so beautiful, Tara. Thank you."

"You're welcome." She plopped onto his lap, snuggling back against his chest. "Tell me a story, Daddy."

Lance smiled. The ruffled seat of her bathing

suit was still wet from her plunge into the water, the sand that clung to her legs and arms gritty against his skin. Nothing had ever felt more wonderful. "Sure, sweetie. Which one would you like to hear?"

"The one 'bout the frog who gets turned into a prince."

"That's your mother's favorite too," he murmured, a smile tugging at his mouth.

The girl giggled. "She says there's a 'portant message in it. But I'd never kiss a yucky old frog."

She shuddered as if imagining it, and Lance laughed. "Speaking of your mother, do you know what she's doing?"

The little girl nodded. "Promised I wouldn't tell, though."

"And I wouldn't want you to." He brushed her downy curls away from her face. "After all, *birthday parties* are supposed to be a surpri—"

"Lancelot Alexander, I can't believe you would stoop so low as to try to trick your own child!"

Father and daughter whipped around to look at the woman walking toward them.

"I didn't tell, Mommy!"

"I know, honey." Madi glared good-naturedly at her husband.

"Can't blame a guy for trying."

Madi placed her hands on her swollen belly. "Especially when there are so many other things to blame him for."

He smiled wickedly. "Gwenn's asleep?"

"Mmm." Madi lowered herself awkwardly to the sand. "Nanny's with her."

"Mommy, Daddy was telling me a story. The one about the frog."

Madi stroked her daughter's arm. "He was?"

"Uh-huh. But I already know how it ends." She popped her thumb into her mouth.

"You do?" Madi asked, amused and, as always, charmed by her daughter. "How's that?"

The thumb came out and the little girl sat up straighter, obviously feeling important and very grown up. "They lived happily ever after."

Madi met Lance's eyes, knowing her own—like his—shone with love and contentment. "The end," she murmured.

THE EDITOR'S CORNER

It's going to be a merry month, indeed, for all of us LOVESWEPT devotees with romances that are charming, delightful, moving, and hot!

First, one of Deborah Smith's most romantic, dreamy love stories ever, CAMELOT, LOVESWEPT #468. Deb sweeps you away to sultry Florida, a setting guaranteed to inspire as much fantasizing in you as it does in heroine Agnes Hamilton. The story opens on a stormy night when Agnes has been thinking and dreaming about the love story recorded in the diary of a knight of Britain's Middle Ages. He seems almost real to her. When the horses on her breeding farm need her help to shelter from the wind and rain, Agnes forges out into the night—only to meet a man on horseback who seems for all the world like her knight of old. Who is the wickedly handsome John Bartholomew and dare she trust their instant attraction to each other? This is a LOVESWEPT to read slowly so you can enjoy each delicious phrase of a beautiful, sensual, exciting story.

Welcome a marvelous new talent to our fold, Virginia Leigh, whose SECRET KEEPER, LOVESWEPT #469, is her first published novel. Heroine Mallory Bennett is beautiful, sexy—and looking her worst in mud-spattered jeans (sounds like real life, huh?), when hero Jake Gallegher spots her in the lobby of his restaurant. From the first he knows she's Trouble . . . and he senses a deep mystery about her. Intrigued, he sets out to probe her secrets and find the way to her heart. Don't miss this moving and thrilling love story by one of our New Faces of '91!

Joan Elliott Pickart is back with a funny, tender, sizzler, MEMORIES, LOVESWEPT #470. This is an irresistible story of a second chance at love for Minty Westerly and Chism Talbert. Minty grew up happy and privileged;

Chism grew up troubled and the caretaker's son. But status and money couldn't come between them for they had all the optimism of the young in love. Then Chism broke Minty's heart, disappearing on the same night they were to elope. Now, back in town, no longer an angry young man, but still full of passion, Chism encounters Minty, a woman made cautious by his betrayal. Their reunion is explosive—full of pain and undimmed passion . . . and real love. You'll revel in the steps this marvelous couple takes along the path to true love!

That marvelous romantic Linda Cajio gives you her best in EARTH ANGEL, LOVESWEPT #471, next month. Heroine Catherine Wagner is a lady with a lot on her mind—rescuing her family business from a ruthless and greedy relative while pursuing the cause of her life. When she meets charismatic banker Miles Kitteridge she thinks he must be too good to be true. His touch, his fleeting kisses leave her weak-kneed. But is he on to her game? And, if so, can she trust him? Miles knows he wants the passionate rebel in his arms forever . . . but capturing her may be the toughest job of his life! A real winner from Linda!

Welcome another one of our fabulous New Faces of '91, Theresa Gladden, with her utterly charming debut novel, ROMANCING SUSAN, LOVESWEPT #472. First, devastatingly handsome Matt Martinelli steals Susan Wright's parking space—then he seems determined to steal her heart! And Susan fears she's just going to be a pushover for his knock-'em-dead grin and gypsy eyes. She resists his lures . . . but when he gains an ally in her matchmaking great aunt, Susan's in trouble—delightfully so. A love story of soft Southern nights and sweet romancing that you'll long remember!

Patt Bucheister strikes again with one of her best ever sensual charmers, HOT PURSUIT, LOVESWEPT #473. Rugged he-man Denver Sierra is every woman's dream and a man who will not take no for an answer. Lucky Courtney Caine! But it takes her a while to realize just how lucky she is. Courtney has hidden in the peaceful shadows cast by her performing family. Denver is determined to draw her out into the bright sunshine of life . . . and to melt her icy fears with the warmth of his affection and the fire of his desire. Bravo, Patt!

We trust that as always you'll find just the romances you want in all six of our LOVESWEPTs next month. Don't forget our new imprint, FANFARE, if you want more of the very best in women's popular fiction. On sale next month from FANFARE are three marvelous novels that we guarantee will keep you riveted. MORTAL SINS is a mesmerizing contemporary novel of family secrets, love, and unforgettable intrigue from a dynamic writing duo, Dianne Edouard and Sandra Ware. THE SCHEMERS by Lois Wolfe is a rich, thrilling historical novel set during the Civil War with the most unlikely—and marvelous—heroine and hero. She's a British aristocrat, he's a half-Apache army scout. Be sure also to put Joan Dial's sweeping historical FROM A FAR COUNTRY on your list of must-buy fiction. This enthralling novel will take you on a romantic journey between continents . . . and the hearts and souls of its unforgettable characters.

Ah, so much for you to look forward to in the merry month ahead.

Warm good wishes,

Carolyn Nichols

Carolyn Nichols
Editor
LOVESWEPT
Bantam Books
666 Fifth Avenue
New York, NY 10102-0023

THE LATEST IN BOOKS
AND AUDIO CASSETTES

Paperbacks

☐	28671	**NOBODY'S FAULT** Nancy Holmes	$5.95
☐	28412	**A SEASON OF SWANS** Celeste De Blasis	$5.95
☐	28354	**SEDUCTION** Amanda Quick	$4.50
☐	28594	**SURRENDER** Amanda Quick	$4.50
☐	28435	**WORLD OF DIFFERENCE** Leonia Blair	$5.95
☐	28416	**RIGHTFULLY MINE** Doris Mortman	$5.95
☐	27032	**FIRST BORN** Doris Mortman	$4.95
☐	27283	**BRAZEN VIRTUE** Nora Roberts	$4.50
☐	27891	**PEOPLE LIKE US** Dominick Dunne	$4.95
☐	27260	**WILD SWAN** Celeste De Blasis	$5.95
☐	25692	**SWAN'S CHANCE** Celeste De Blasis	$5.95
☐	27790	**A WOMAN OF SUBSTANCE** Barbara Taylor Bradford	$5.95

Audio

☐ **SEPTEMBER** by Rosamunde Pilcher
Performance by Lynn Redgrave
180 Mins. Double Cassette   45241-X $15.95

☐ **THE SHELL SEEKERS** by Rosamunde Pilcher
Performance by Lynn Redgrave
180 Mins. Double Cassette   48183-9 $14.95

☐ **COLD SASSY TREE** by Olive Ann Burns
Performance by Richard Thomas
180 Mins. Double Cassette   45166-9 $14.95

☐ **NOBODY'S FAULT** by Nancy Holmes
Performance by Geraldine James
180 Mins. Double Cassette   45250-9 $14.95